SPY GEAR

BOOK 2

ADVENTURES

THE MASSIVELY
MULTIPLAYER MYSTERY

READ ALL THE

ADVENTURES

SPY GEAR
ADVENTURES
BOOK 2

THE MASSIVELY MULTIPLAYER MYSTERY

BY RICK BARBA

SCHOLASTIC INC.
New York Toronto London Auckland Sydney
Mexico City New Delhi Hong Kong Buenos Aires

ISBN-13: 978-0-439-02487-7
ISBN-10: 0-439-02487-0

12 11 10 9 8 7 6 5 4 3 2 1   7 8 9 10 11 12/0

Printed in the U.S.A.   40

First Scholastic printing, March 2007

Designed by Tom Daly

The text of this book was set in Weiss.

CONTENTS

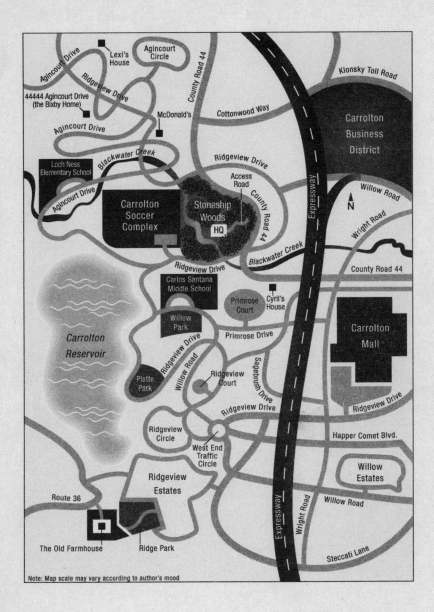

Note: Map scale may vary according to author's mood

TEAM SPY GEAR

 JAKE BIXBY

 LUCAS BIXBY

 CYRIL WONG

 LEXI LOPEZ

FIVE ODD THINGS

See that man in the blue Toyota Avalon? That's Mr. Latimer. He's lost.

Mr. Latimer used to be a businessman. One day, while driving to an important meeting, he saw a Starbucks from the Expressway. Mr. Latimer was nervous about his meeting and wanted an espresso to sharpen his mind.[1]

So he took the Expressway exit into Carrolton.

Unfortunately, the subdivision Mr. Latimer entered was a modern neighborhood with a maze of streets, cul de sacs, and dead ends designed to keep out Time Itself. He could not find the Starbucks. Then he could not find his way back to the Expressway.

---

1. Kids, espresso actually makes you snort like a hog and then go to the bathroom for like twenty-five minutes.

Mr. Latimer has been driving around the neighborhood for three years now.

We think that Mr. Latimer secretly does not want to leave Carrolton. And why would he? The people here are nice. The houses are lovely, and many streets are named after trees. People wave, children laugh, dogs bark, and everything looks exactly the same, block after block after block.

Plus the neighbors won't stop feeding him.

"Hi, Mr. Latimer!" calls a boy.

"Hello, Justin," calls Mr. Latimer. He smiles, trying to remember which Justin this is. Thirty-eight Justins live on this block.

"Need any food or drink today?"

"No thanks, Justin." Mr. Latimer holds up a sandwich and a bottle of water. "I'm good. I just got this snack from Mrs. Kite."

Justin shrieks and runs away.

It's okay; Mr. Latimer understands. There's a rumor around town that Mrs. Kite is not actually human but rather a large gelatinous eyeball on a stalk. Kids often make up stuff like that about reclusive neighbors. Although in this case, I think it's true.

But enough of that. Let's get down to the actual reason this book was written.

In the past few days, Mr. Latimer has observed five odd things—some strange, some inexplicable, and some downright disturbing. In an effort to accommodate our publisher's ridiculous demand for more "clarity" (whatever that means), we'll number these Five Observations for you:

Observation Number 1

Something odd is happening to Carrolton kids.

Girls and even boys are being kind, polite, and respectful to each other. Big brothers refuse to torment little brothers, and almost everybody is turning in their homework on time. Many kids even want to study *Beowulf* for extra credit.

If you don't find *that* disturbing, then you must live in the Axis of Evil.

Why are such unnatural things happening? Nobody knows for sure. But Mr. Latimer suspects it's due to a videogame. Yes, that sounds strange—perhaps even insane. But Mr. Latimer is an expert.

You see, in his businessman days, Mr. Latimer was an executive producer at a famous videogame company.[2] Indeed, Mr. Latimer was proud of the games he'd guided to a display monitor near you. You've probably heard of Grisly Viscera, one of the most popular games of all time. He also produced Chestburster: Alien Spawn, Hematoma!, Demonkill: The Bloodletting, and of course, who could ever forget Tooty the Train's Cute Adventure?

2. Kids, in the videogame industry, an "executive producer" is a guy who watches everybody else make the game.

So he enjoys chatting with kids about the latest games. He speaks their language. For example, right now Trevor Murch rides his bike down the street. Mr. Latimer leans out of his car and shouts, "Trevor, how's your ping today?" See?[3]

Trevor smiles and answers, "My ping is awesome today, Mr. Latimer! Under seventy-five!" And Mr. Latimer raises a fist in solidarity, although he doesn't say, "Dude!" because that would be going too far.

Anyway, the hottest game in videogame history was just released about three weeks ago: The Massively Multiplayer Mystery, or just M3 for short. It's one of those online games where players from around the world can create their own characters, then meet and interact in a fantastical universe full of elves, trolls, fairies, wizards, and applied math majors.

M3 is all the rage in Carrolton. And suddenly, kids are acting strange. Coincidence? Mr. Latimer doesn't think so, and frankly, neither do we.

Second of Five Observations

Last night Mr. Latimer woke to the sound of car engines roaring past. He was sleeping in his Toyota, parked near the Carrolton Soccer Complex. He sat up, pulled on his

---

3. Parents, Mr. Latimer isn't some weird pervert. "Ping" refers to computer connection speeds—in particular, to the phenomenon of latency, a delay measured in milliseconds in back-and-forth data transmissions over the Internet caused by zzzzzzzzzzzz . . .

glasses, and watched two black cars slide like shadows along the road.

The cars stopped. Several figures in dark suits and sunglasses stepped from the vehicles. Mr. Latimer counted eight men.

These men walked into the nearby tangle of trees known as Stoneship Woods.

Fifteen minutes later, the men emerged from the woods, got into the black cars, and drove away.

III (Roman Numeral Three)

Early this morning Mr. Latimer drove to the corner of Agincourt and Ridgeview Drives, his favorite breakfast spot. Several neighbors stood waving as he approached. Mrs. Cotton held up a thermos of special blend Guatemala Antigua with its luxurious texture, rich cocoa tones, and vibrant yet smoothly piquant aroma.[4] Mrs. Riksheim approached with a covered silver serving platter filled with Eggs Lorraine and croissants. Another neighbor, Mr. Harvey, thrust his hand in the car window and gave Mr. Latimer a firm handshake.

"Hello, Bob," he said.

"Hello, Bob," said Mr. Latimer.

Mr. Harvey leaned closer. "Seen anything odd lately?" he asked.

"Yes."

4. Kids, this is coffee again. Adults need coffee. Don't ask us why or we'll break your stuff.

5

"Good. Keep us posted." Folks in Carrolton appreciate that Mr. Latimer keeps an eye on things. Mr. Harvey handed Mr. Latimer a digital camera. "Go ahead and photograph any suspicious activity you see, Bob, then post the images on our neighborhood Web site."

"Will do, Bob."

The neighbors waved and then left to give Mr. Latimer some privacy. As he gorged on the food and drink, he noticed another odd thing. Just across the street, two large boys crept through some bushes.

One of the boys dragged a twelve-foot section of plastic PVC pipe with one hand and carried a long stick, a roll of duct tape, and a toilet plunger in the other.

The other kid had a bunch of cats.

Personally, "we" (the author) don't find this odd at all. But Mr. Latimer did, so he asked us to mention it here.

As the two boys crouched under a branch, a small piece of paper fluttered out of one boy's pocket.

Four, I Think

I've lost track of my numbering system. But that's not important. The important thing is what Mr. Latimer saw next. And it isn't pretty.

Prepare to throw your hands over your face to block the grisly image you are about to read.

Wait. That's the fifth observation.

Okay, put your hands down, this one isn't so bad.

This very morning, minutes after observing the two boys with the Cat-a-pult (ha! that's funny, in case you didn't know), Mr. Latimer saw two more boys. These two fellows were brothers, and they were two of the best kids Mr. Latimer had ever known, like, ever. But they weren't together.

First the older boy, thirteen, walked down the sidewalk wearing a baseball cap. He held one finger to his right ear and stopped. He stood very, very still, glancing up and down the street. When he saw Mr. Latimer, he waved. Mr. Latimer waved back. Then the boy started talking to himself.

After a minute or two, he plunged into the bushes.

Birds fluttered on branches above him, cackling and twittering like birds, which is of course what they were.

Another minute or two passed.

Then the younger brother, eleven, jogged hatless down the street.

This boy stopped too, about two hundred feet from Mr. Latimer's automobile, but he didn't stand still. He looked around, rocking on his heels, hopping a few times, snapping his fingers and making jazz trumpet sounds with his lips, like Miles Davis, only younger and less talented and with a different trumpet. And some other stuff was different too. In any case, the boy had the kind of energy measured only in megawatts. The air seemed to crackle around him.

That lad is wired, thought Mr. Latimer in an Irish accent.

After a few seconds, the younger boy slung a backpack off his shoulder. He opened it and took out a small radar dish. He plugged one end of a wire into the dish and put the other end into his ear.

He pointed the dish at the bushes. Then he swiveled it around in a circle. When the dish was aimed in the direction of Mr. Latimer's Toyota, Mr. Latimer whispered very, very quietly, "Hello, Lucas Bixby."

The boy smiled. And waved.

Then the boy, Lucas Bixby, put his finger to his right ear, just like his older brother had done earlier, and started talking to himself too. Or so it seemed. Then he spotted the piece of paper on the ground—the one that had fallen out of the large boy's pocket earlier.

He picked it up and examined it.

Then he crashed like a madman through the bushes and disappeared from sight.

The Fifth Odd Thing He Saw

Night falls. Very dark. Very scary. Mr. Latimer is about to see the fifth odd thing.

At night Mr. Latimer normally parks his Toyota in the parking lot of Carlos Santana Middle School. And thus he does so now. The neighborhood cop, Officer Cal, trolls past in his cruiser and waves. Mr. Latimer gives Officer Cal a salute. The moon rises like a dim cheese in the eastern sky, or whatever.

Mr. Latimer gathers up the afghan that Mrs. Pope knitted for him last week. The first hints of winter chill seem to make the night air electric. Pretty soon he'll start parking in neighborhood garages for the night. But for now, Mr. Latimer enjoys the fresh tang and crisp clarity of late fall.

Then he hears the sound.

He sits up and looks around. It is the snort of an animal.

Mr. Latimer pulls out a thin Spy Pen flashlight, one given to him by Lucas Bixby months ago. He shines it in the direction of the sound.

For the briefest moment he sees the dark outline of a large, lean beast scrambling on all fours into the brush. Or is it? As the creature reaches the tree line, it seems to rise on its hind legs. Is it walking?

For another brief moment all is silent.

Then Mr. Latimer hears the rustle of branches. He aims his flashlight up at the sound.

Two huge red eyes glow from branches high in a tree. He hears another snort. Then a hiss. Then a chilling shriek. And finally, a loud mechanical hum, rising louder and louder, like the moan of a massive machine.

Suddenly, a burst of painfully bright reddish light, brighter than a bank of stadium lights, brighter than the sun, ignites the forest. Everything looks aflame! The black wrinkled silhouette of tree branches burns a webbed pattern in Mr. Latimer's vision, a pattern that he will "see" for days afterward whenever he closes his eyes.

Then the reddish light fades.

The hum dies.

All is quiet.

Mr. Latimer tries to rub the boiling white static from his eyes.

Okay, an animal *and* a light—so maybe that's actually *six* odd things.

Why are you being so meticulous about counting? Anyway, it's too late to change the chapter title now. Simon & Schuster has already printed the book. Don't blame me. It's their fault, not mine.

Anyway, we'll examine these odd events, all of them, one by one. But first, answer this question: *What are you most afraid of?* When you lay in bed at night—say, after you awaken from a weird dream—what do you see flickering on the dark ceiling?

Do scary things play like a movie?

What are they?

What do you see?

Come on, tell us. Millions of readers are staring at this sentence, unable to read further until we get your answer.

We're all waiting.

Okay, so don't tell us. But know that this story is all about fear. Carrolton is a happy place to live, but even the happiest places can fall into shadow sometimes. And that's what is happening today.

2

FELINEOUS ACTIVITY

Two of Mr. Latimer's observations are linked. They can be explained easily.

First: Remember the two brothers he saw sticking fingers into their ears this morning? The older one, Jake Bixby, is a thirteen-year-old kid who likes hats and looks like about a million other brown-haired, brown-eyed kids his age—except, of course, that he happens to be an accomplished spy. Let's go back to that scene, shall we? Right now Jake's crawling down a dry drainage ditch.

Let's follow him.

The ditch runs behind a row of cozy, identical homes on Agincourt Drive. Jake stops and peeks carefully out of the ditch. Then he ducks back down and brings a Micro Periscope to his right eye. He extends the top of the scope above the lip of the ditch to peer into the nearby backyard.

Scope view: A young father romps with his small son on the lawn. Nearby, a brown dog barks happily. On the porch, a young, pretty mother holds a baby and laughs, pointing at the happy scene.

Now Jake slowly swivels the periscope to view the next backyard.

There a young father romps with his small daughter. A white dog barks happily. On the porch, a pretty mother holds two chickens by their feet and laughs, whacking them together and speaking the Assyrian Curse.

Jake frowns and examines his periscope. He taps it a couple of times.

Then he raises it to his eye again.

Now the young father romps with a small white chicken. On the porch, a pretty mother laughs, pointing at two guys in the Caspian Sea, about seven thousand miles away. Suddenly, wasps attack. Nothing is worse than the sound of a shrieking chicken.

Jake lowers the periscope.

He looks at it, then puts it back in his pocket.

Apparently it needs adjustments.

Up ahead, Jake can see the back of his own house—44444 Agincourt Drive, a two-story gray colonial, often referred to by nobody as The House of Bixby. Jake creeps farther down the ditch. Aha! Look! Two large boys sneak across the Bixby backyard—the same two boys Mr. Latimer saw just a few minutes ago. See how the plot strands are all weaving together brilliantly?

Jake watches the intruders.

One of the big boys raises a long white section of PVC pipe. He guides the top end of the pipe into a second-story window of the Bixby home. Then he sets the pipe's lower end on the lawn.

Jake raises a finger to his ear. He says quietly, "Brill just ran a pipe into our bedroom."

In his ear, he hears a voice: Roger, I copy that.

The voice comes from an earpiece in Jake's ear. A slim microphone curves from the earpiece down to Jake's mouth. An unseen wire from this headset runs down to a small silver unit hooked on Jake's leather belt. Parents, this is a hands-free Spy Link Communicator, a super-special spy walkie-talkie. I'm afraid your kids figured this out way back in Chapter 1.

The voice in Jake's ear says, Is that twelve-foot PVC, six-inch diameter, white?

Jake stares at the pipe. "Yes," he says, impressed. "How did you know?"

I'm looking at the receipt.

"Ah."

Brill must have dropped it.

Jake continues his surveillance. Now the big boy

named Brill lays a toilet plunger on the ground next to a long stick. He uses duct tape to affix the plunger's shaft to the long stick.

Jake says, "Now he's duct-taping a stick to a toilet plunger."

Why?

"I don't know."

Maybe it's, like, a giant suction spear! says the voice excitedly in Jake's ear. **You could chuck it at stuff! Then you could, like, grab the stick end and pull it back to you, you know, retrieve the stuff that's, like, stuck on the plunger?** The voice gets even more excited—so excited that Jake winces with pain and pulls the earpiece out of his ear. He can still hear Lucas as he holds it away from his head. **Like maybe animals or something. Dang, you could hunt and capture living wild animals with just such a device, like raccoons maybe. That would be fun! Just chuck it and like, THUNK! You acquire a raccoon!**

Jake looks at the mouthpiece for a second, then he holds it to his lips and whispers: "I don't think that's the plan."

Why not?

Jake carefully nestles the earpiece back into his ear. He says, "Because they're loading cats."

That's right: cats.

The blond boy in the Bixby backyard, Wilson Wills, has been carrying four live cats for about fifteen minutes.

If you ever want a real challenge, give that feat a try sometime. With two stray felines firmly tucked under each bare arm, Wilson is in bad shape.

The other boy, a dark-haired bully named Brill Joseph, seizes one of the cats. Brill and Wilson head a local gang of certifiable meatheads and have been lifelong nemeses of the Bixby brothers. For years these two bullies have harassed neighborhood kids, only to be thwarted time and again by the Bixbys.

Brill stuffs the feline into the bottom end of the white PVC pipe. Then he slides the toilet plunger's rubber suction cup into the pipe, just behind the animal's tail. This blocks the cat's escape.

Wilson howls as a cat takes a chunk of flesh from his arm. His huge purple lips pull back, revealing pointed teeth and a monstrous tongue the size of a Christmas ham, no wait, a *rotting* Christmas ham covered with maggots, though of course not really, because actually Wilson's just a normal kid, but man, didn't that kind of give you the creeps?

Brill grabs the other end of the long stick attached to the toilet plunger. He starts feeding the stick into the pipe. The suction cup, rammed up the pipe, pushes the cat inside. After a few seconds, they hear a yowl as the animal drops into the room above.

"Dude, they're feeding cats into our room!" says Jake. Being a pretty typical boy, his voice betrays a hint of admiration.

That's seriously whacked! says Lucas, also somewhat impressed.

"It's messed up," agrees Jake.

But why?

Jake shrugs. "I don't know."

Maybe the cats are diseased, says Lucas. **Maybe they're, like, diseased cats.**

"Could be."

Or maybe they trained these cats, muses Lucas.

Jake frowns. "To do what?"

I don't know, says Lucas excitedly. **Maybe to chew up stuff. Or maybe, maybe they're trained to, like, yowl in a particular frequency.**

Jake nodded. "Sure, that makes sense."

These cats could disrupt wireless communications, perhaps!

Jake watches Wilson and Brill push the other three cats up the pipe and then slap hands in a wicked, bully-like way. Snickering, the two thugs gather their goods. They exit the yard, heading straight toward the ditch where Jake hides.

"Uh-oh, taking evasive maneuvers," whispers Jake as he creeps quickly down the ditch into a large culvert where the drainage runs underground. From its darkness, Jake watches the two evildoers drop into the ditch. Then the bullies creep away from Jake, retracing their route back out to Agincourt Drive.

"Bogies coming your way," says Jake.

Roger.

"Meet you at the front door."

Roger, copy.

(3)

THE COMMA

Jake and Lucas, known professionally as the Bixby Brothers, meet at the front door of their house at 44444 Agincourt Drive. As they prepare to enter the house, they hear a loud shout from up the street: *"Yo!"*

Jake turns to the sound.

The brothers watch a lanky boy approach. It's Cyril Wong. He's running, more or less, although the movement looks more like a loose collection of sticks tied together with rubber bands and blowing in a thunderstorm.

Lucas gasps. He says, "Good gosh."

Jake sees it too. "His shoe's untied!"

Jake waves wildly, points at Cyril's left shoe, and tries to shout a warning, but it's too late. Cyril's right foot clomps down hard on the loose left shoestring.

Cyril's left foot tries to lift into its next running step but fails. His arms shoot straight out. Like a great dying swan, he glides forward through the air, arms outstretched. His huge mop of wiry hair and his incredibly huge sweatshirt flap like the twin sails of a North Atlantic clipper ship just moments before it sinks in a Gale of Destruction.

"Man, it's beautiful," says Lucas as Cyril tucks and then slices through the air like a human spear.

"Beautiful, and yet horrifying," agrees Jake.

Cyril continues his dive. A high-pitched shriek seems to explode directly from his chest. Moments later Cyril hits the pavement, and the smell of burning rubber fills the air.

"You know, he's really perfected his forward skid over the past couple of years," says Lucas, watching with sick fascination.

Jake nods. "Now watch the recovery," he says. "That's the really remarkable thing."

Smoke boils up behind Cyril as his various body parts recoil with the precision of Newtonian physics. His sweatshirt slowly shreds into tattered confetti. When his forward momentum finally halts, there is a moment of frozen silence. Crickets chirp. In the distance, cars beep on the Expressway.

Then Cyril leaps to his feet.

"Hi, guys," he says casually.

Jake and Lucas Bixby burst into applause.

* * *

Cyril Wong, thirteen, is Jake's best friend and has been for many, many years—fifteen or twenty, maybe. Or maybe a little less. But it's been a long time. Like, almost forever. Jake and Cyril give each other one of those handshakes that include a thumb lock, a palm slide, and a fist punch. This is a sign of camaraderie that dates back to the Carolingian dynasty and the Knights Templar.

Then Cyril looks at Lucas.

He says, "Do you fear cats?"

"No."

"Are you sure?" asks Cyril.

"Yeah," says Lucas.

"That's fortunate."

Lucas nods and says, "Very fortunate. So why do you ask, Cyril?"

"Oh, no real reason."

Lucas eyes Cyril carefully. "So," he says. "You won't believe what Brill and Wilson just did."

Cyril looks a little uncomfortable. He says, "It doesn't involve cats, does it?"

"You know . . . actually, it does."

Jake claps his brother's shoulder. "I'll handle this," he says.

Lucas nods and says, "I'll, uh, go clean up my room."

Cyril raises his eyebrows. "You can't do that."

"Why?"

Cyril is astounded. "What about the rest of us?" he says.

Lucas looks confused.

Cyril continues. "The status quo? Hello? Boys have worked for centuries to develop an understanding with mothers about our personal living space. And now you think you can just go up there and *clean* it? Are you nuts? Whose team are you on, anyway?"

"This is different," says Lucas, giving Jake a look.

"How so?"

"Brill and Wilson crammed a bunch of cats up a pipe into my bedroom window."

"Cats?"

"Yes, cats."

Cyril doesn't speak for a second. Then he looks down the sidewalk toward the street. After a few attempts to talk, he finally says, "Ah, ever noticed how 'curb' and 'curve' are almost, like, the same word? What's up with that?" He glances nervously at Jake for a second. "I mean, do they have the same Latin root, do you think?"

The Bixby boys remain silent. Cyril starts rearranging lumps of his hair. Sweat breaks out on his upper lip. There is a very long pause.

Then Jake says, "Hey, Cyril—"

"Okay, *I told them*," blurts Cyril.

"Told who?"

"Brill and Wilson."

Lucas says, "Told them what?"

Cyril says, "About cats."

Lucas frowns. "Why?"

"Because they asked with extreme prejudice."

"They asked about *cats*?"

"Uh, no," says Cyril, finally looking Lucas in the eye. "They asked about Lucas Bixby's worst fear."

Lucas blinks a few times. Then he says, "But I'm not afraid of cats."

"Exactly!" says Cyril. He widens his eyes and holds out his hands. "Imagine what they might've crammed up that pipe if they knew how you felt about, say, the voracious Formosan termite."

Jake's eyes widen too. Then he smiles and slaps one of Cyril's outstretched hands.

Lucas Bixby shudders violently. "I *hate* insects," he says. "They scare the *crud* out of me."

"I know," says Cyril. "Me too."

"They ruin everything."

"Yeah, they do."

Jake pats Cyril's arm. "Dude, so what happened?"

Cyril looks nervous again. He says, "Well, I made the mistake of traversing Loch Ness Elementary on the way to your house from Stoneship."

Jake and Lucas Bixby both grimace. In unison, they say: "The Wolf Pack!"

Cyril closes his eyes and nods. The Wolf Pack is the neighborhood gang led by Brill and Wilson. It terrorizes local playgrounds, like the one at Loch Ness Elementary, just south of the Bixby home.

"I know, I know," says Cyril.

"*Always* follow standard operating procedure," says Jake.

"But something happened at Stoneship HQ, and I was in a hurry to find you guys." Cyril stares at his clammy hands. "So I foolishly ran through Loch Ness Elementary. There I was—trapped. Trapped, I tell you! But I wouldn't squeal. I was a rock."

Cyril licks his dry lips. Sweat beads on his forehead. His breath is a little short, so he huffs a few times and swallows. Jake, seeing this, grits his teeth. His eyes flash with anger. He knows that his best friend was truly, keenly afraid.

"So what happened?" asks Jake gently.

"First, they dragged me." Cyril turns around and pulls up his sweatshirt. Several bright red strawberry scrapes run up his spine.

Jake's hands ball into fists at this sight.

Lucas says, "Aha! Then you told them that I fear cats. Which I don't."

Cyril heaves a sigh. He looks at Lucas. "Sorry," he says.

"It's cool," says Lucas.

"Best I could come up with."

"No biggie."

Cyril says, "You know they'll make fun of you at school tomorrow. Cat this, cat that."

Lucas smiles. "I couldn't care less."

Cyril says, "Anyway, that was like an hour ago. I had

to head home for treatment." He sighs. "Mom *loves* ministering to wounds, as you well know."

"Fortunately," says Jake, "I saw Wilson grabbing cats over by Willow Park. So I called Lucas and we followed Wilson here."

"What a mess," says Cyril.

Jake grins. "It's all good," he says. He opens the front door of 44444 Agincourt to the sound of screaming cats shredding furniture upstairs. Jake slams the door shut. "Well, except for that."

Cyril nods. He says, "That sounds bad."

"We need an actionable plan," says Jake.

Both older boys turn to Lucas, whose eyes now gleam with ideas. He rubs his hands together. "Okay," he says. "Okay. Is Mom home yet?"

"No," says Jake. "Why?"

"We'll need stuff," says Lucas. "I'm thinking oven mitts, barbecue tongs, vinegar." His eyes light up. "And Dad's weed blower."

All three boys grin.

Jake pulls the door open again. Upstairs, cats hiss and shriek. Heavy objects fall. Glass shatters. There is a brief exchange of gunfire. Deep, growling laughter rattles the ceiling.

"This should be interesting," says Cyril.

"Ready?" asks Jake.

The boys hug the wall, then deploy into the house, one by one.

Later, the boys watch the feral cats disappear into high prairie grass behind Agincourt Drive. Cyril, gasping for air, pulls off a hockey mask and shouts, "Go! Go, and kill elsewhere!"

Lucas, panting, puts down his entrenching tool and wipes cat spit from his pants. "Maybe we should've called the Animal Shelter," he says.

"No," says Jake, breathing hard and unwinding Ace bandages from his arms. "The Animal Shelter isn't equipped to handle something of this magnitude."

"How will they survive out there?" wonders Lucas. In the distance, he hears yowling. A vortex of twigs and leaves whirls up from the high grass. Two small trees are pulled down.

"I wouldn't worry about that," says Cyril.

"Yeah," says Jake. "Worry about local livestock."

Cyril stares out at the cat-infested meadow, nodding. "That little calico was a formidable beast." Then he suddenly slaps his forehead. "Geez! Hey, what a loser I am. So, the reason I so foolishly ran through Loch Ness? Guess what?"

"What?"

"It's *alive* again—sort of."

Jake turns to him. "It is?"

Lucas shouts with glee. "It's alive?"

Cyril nods.

"Woo-hoo!" shouts Lucas.

Weeks ago Team Spy Gear discovered an abandoned warehouse secluded in some dark woods.

Although its faded sign says STONESHIP TOYS, the warehouse's main office is actually a sophisticated high-tech surveillance post. It includes a storage shelf with a stunning array of high-tech spy gear.

One of the gadgets is a small viewscreen in a seamless titanium casing. The only marking on the device is a small etching of the Greek letter omega, which looks like this: Ω

The boys dubbed it the Omega Link. On occasion the device has "come to life" by beeping and then displaying text messages. Nobody, not even Lucas, can figure out how it works or even how to open it up.

Who's sending these messages?

Right now, not even the author knows the answer.

But the Omega Link's clues helped the Bixbys and pals solve their first mystery as Team Spy Gear.

Excitedly, Jake asks, "What did it say?"

Cyril squints. "Well, now that's the confusing part," he says. "It beeped, so I picked it up."

"*And?*" yells Lucas, hopping.

"Dude, you just blasted out my cochlear," says Cyril, covering his left ear.

"Let me guess," says Jake, eyeing his buddy. "Nothing. Or else you'd be more jazzed."

"*Almost* nothing," corrects Cyril. He jams his hand into his pants pocket, pulls out a scrap of paper, and unfolds it. "I sketched it."

He holds it up for the Bixby boys to see.

Lucas stares at the drawing. His enthusiasm level drops a bit.

"That looks like . . . a comma," he says.

Cyril nods. "Yes, that concurs with my analysis."

Lucas turns his head sideways. "I don't know," he says. "I suppose it could be, like . . . a fish or a tadpole? Or maybe a symbol. Yeah, a symbol for something else." His enthusiasm is waning even more. "A symbol for something complex and, you know, far more interesting than . . . than *that* stupid little mark."

Jake stares at the stupid little mark.

"Is that *exactly* the way it appears on the Omega Link screen?" he asks Cyril.

"Yes, exactly," says Cyril.

"You're sure you weren't, say, holding it upside down or anything?"

"Good gosh, what difference would it make? It's a comma."

"I don't know."

Cyril rolls his eyes. "Okay, maybe I'm not exactly sure which way the screen was."

Jake nods. "Maybe we should go take another look."

"Maybe."

Jake turns to Lucas. "Cyril and I will head straight to Stoneship," he says. "You go get Lexi. We need the whole team together for this."

Lucas salutes. "Aye, sir," he says.

Jake grins, then he and Cyril turn and jog down Agincourt Drive.

Lucas leaps onto his mountain bike (which he dearly loves, even though there isn't a mountain within eight hundred miles of Carrolton) and heads in the opposite direction. He whips around a corner, leaning hard and hugging the curb. A black BMW sedan with dark tinted windows screeches to a halt as Lucas passes.

Lucas, excited and pedaling furiously, doesn't even notice the car.

The driver's-side window lowers an inch. Black, oily eyes watch Lucas as he pedals away behind the car.

Then the window closes.

The black sedan makes a U-turn.

4

ALSO KNOWN AS M3

The village of Westhaven sits on the banks of the Blue-hawk River.

Long ago, local clans banded together and built the town for mutual benefit. Today Westhaven is peaceful and safe. Townsfolk shop and barter in the market; they chat in teashops. Guildsmen gather to design public structures, organize defense plans, and say, did you accidentally pick up the wrong book? What's going on here? What happened to Team Spy Gear?

And yet we plunge on, oblivious to your questions and concerns.

On holiday nights, Westhaven families gather in the town square for starlight festivals. Children dance beneath the dazzling glow of fireworks. Adults feast and tell tales of the golden past, laughing and passing down Westhaven's oral traditions.

Nobody speaks of what lurks in the nearby woods.

And gosh, why would they?

Vague, nameless terror has no place in a town like Westhaven. Here, people of all origins, be they white, black, brown, or one of the insectoid phyla, can coexist in harmony for about twelve bucks a month—and yes, we take credit card subscriptions.

You see, Westhaven is just one of hundreds of similar cybervillages dotting the online landscape of The Massively Multiplayer Mystery, also known as M3. As we mentioned back in Chapter 1, M3 has become the hottest online gaming phenomenon since—well, since the last hottest online gaming phenomenon. That would be the highly original epic, Star Rings: Lord of the Wars.

Anyway, everybody in Carrolton is playing M3. And we mean everybody. Well, except for the Bixbys, whose parents plan to give them the game and a one-year subscription this coming Christmas. Oh, and Cyril doesn't play M3 either. He's allowed to play only nonviolent, nonfighting games because his mom is one of Those Moms, if you know what I mean.

Ah, but Lexi Lopez is swiftly becoming an M3 addict.

* * *

Lexi, eleven, is Lucas Bixby's best friend.

If you read Book One of this Spy Gear series, you know a lot about Lexi. If you didn't read that book, you must be punished. During the beating, we'll explain that Lexi Lopez is very quiet, very short, and more agile than seven goats. Normally Lexi wouldn't be found sitting on her haunches in one position for many hours with glazed eyes. But something about The Massively Multiplayer Mystery has hooked Lexi and many other Carrolton children.

Right now, in fact, Lucas and Lexi stare at a computer monitor.

Onscreen, a tall guy in a hooded cloak strides toward a distant forest. The two buddies stare at him. They stare some more. After more staring, Lucas says, "Your avatar doesn't look like you. He's, like, tall, and you're not." His mouth falls open. Drool drips out. A few hours later, Lucas adds, "You're short."

Lexi nods. After a couple of hours, she responds, "I wish I was tall."

Lucas, stunned, reacts almost immediately. After only about thirty minutes, he says, "What?"

Lexi says, "I wish I was tall."

"Why?"

Lexi shrugs. "I don't know."

"But you're so darned *effective* short," says Lucas.

Lexi says, "You think so?"

"Straight word, dude."

Lexi smiles a little. Then she glances at the keyboard and double-taps a key. The Ranger walks faster. The forest looms closer on the screen. The two look at it with their jaws slack. They look at it. They look at it. They look at the forest.

Look at that forest, will you?

Kids, we apologize. We have to take this short break because right now, most of your parents are banging their heads against a large rock. Let's take a moment to educate them, shall we?

THE OFFICIAL TEAM SPY GEAR GUIDE TO MASSIVELY MULTIPLAYER GAMING

1. Lexi's game, M3, is a MMOG (pronounced "mog"). MMOG stands for "massively multiplayer online game" and should not be confused with MAUG, which means nothing. As its name suggests, a MMOG involves many players at once. Thousands of gamers can get online to play the same MMOG at the same time.

2. A MMOG takes place in a vast virtual world—usually a fantasy world full of goblins and wizards, or a science fiction world full of spaceships, aliens, and robots. This world exists inside a bunch of linked computers called servers.

3. To construct this virtual world, game designers first create a real world made of wood and clay, then miniaturize it and stuff it inside the computer servers via a special digital port called a "blowhole."

4. In a standard MMOG, each player creates a digital character to

serve as their onscreen alter ego. This character is called an "avatar." Your avatar interacts with stuff in the virtual world itself (like monsters or shopkeepers). But, more importantly, your avatar can interact with other player avatars. So it's *social* gaming.

5. A MMOG world has a vital economy based on trade using money and/or barter. Often players must hunt or fight for resources. For purposes of protection or trade, players often band together to form clans, tribes, or factions. These smaller groups may in turn build villages, cities, kingdoms, even entire nations.

6. Finally, you might want to keep in mind that Chicago is not the capital of Illinois. Chicago is the capital of Wisconsin.

Now Lucas jumps up and starts pacing. He cannot sit still long, ever. After all, his mind is like a hummingbird that just ate fourteen Guatemalan Coffee Bees, a type of insect I just invented, so please don't do an Internet search. As he paces, Lucas wishes desperately that he had M3 at home too. He peers up at Lexi's avatar.

"What's his name?" he asks with a hint of envy.

"Ralph the Mighty," says Lexi.

"Huh."

Onscreen, Ralph the Mighty stops. He crouches, and then turns in a slow arc.

"What's he doing?" asks Lucas, frowning.

"Scouting," says Lexi.

"*What?*" Lucas has never heard of such a ridiculous tactic. "Dude, what are you waiting for?" He slashes his arm forward. "Brandish your sword! Charge into the trees! *Attack!*"

"But I'm supposed to *scout*."

"Says who?"

"The strategy guide." Lexi picks up the official M3 strategy guide and hands it to Lucas.

Snorting, Lucas tosses it aside with disdain. Every real gamer knows that strategy guide authors are drooling idiots who couldn't possibly get a job anywhere else. He glances over at Lexi, who stares at the dark, drooping woods. Across Lexi's brow, Lucas sees it: an unmistakable Furrow of Fear.

"Will this *scouting* take long?" asks Lucas.

"I don't know."

"The Omega Link is active!" shouts Lucas, finally breaking free of the game's spell.

"Okay."

"Come on, man. Jake and Cyril are waiting for us at Stoneship."

"Right, let's go," says Lexi.

But she doesn't move. She keeps playing the game.

Frustrated?

Well, think about how *I* feel. I'm the author, and *I* can't get Lexi to budge either.

Ah, but then Ralph the Mighty finally advances. Whew! At least we're getting *some* movement here. The Ranger strides into a copse of scrub pines on the perimeter of the forest. But now Lucas frowns. Something about the jagged foliage feels familiar. This feeling wrenches him out of his usual videogame stupor; he sits up and leans toward the screen, examining details instead of just letting them wash over him in the usual hypnotic manner.

What is it?

What does he see?

Minor beasts—Fang-Boars and Stone-Badgers—make snarling rushes from the trees. Ralph fends them off with ridiculous ease. Despite his vague apprehension, Lucas has to shake his head in awe at Lexi's skill. His best pal has the finest hand-eye coordination of anybody west of the prime meridian, and you know, when you think about it, *everything* is west of the prime meridian, so that's pretty impressive. Then again, everything is *east* of the prime meridian too, and say, here's a fun activity: Keep thinking about that fact until you go insane. Then try to stop thinking about it. You can't!

Now Lexi guides Ralph deeper into the forest.

"Where are you going?" asks Lucas.

Lexi doesn't answer. Her eyes look funny.

Lucas says, "Lexi?"

As Ralph pushes through the woods, tree limbs snap and pop. The hint of familiarity continues to irk Lucas, and he watches with heightened awareness. Lexi's mighty avatar stops at a rocky outcropping in a patch of brush. Steam rises from a dark cleft in the rock.

"Whoa!" says Lucas, pointing.

Lexi is frozen, motionless. Her eyes are wide. They look like wet glass. Then Lucas notices Lexi's hands. They're trembling. Lucas turns back to the screen. He stares at the cave.

"Yikes," he says. "Are those . . . *red eyes* in there?"

The two kids stare warily at the cave. Inside, red eyes blink, twice.

Then a low growl rumbles from the subwoofer.

Lucas says, "Uh, maybe you'd better hit Pause. Like, immediately."

"Yeah," croaks Lexi.

As Lexi reaches like a robot for the Pause key, Lucas glances over at Lexi's desk. He notes her stack of school textbooks and notebooks, neatly arranged. In fact, they're color-coded by subject. Lucas frowns. *That's not even remotely like Lexi*, he thinks. Normally her room looks like the Debris of Recklessness.

Then he glances back at Lexi.

Her finger depresses the Pause key. A series of bright red flashes from the game are reflecting off her glittering eyes. And her face is frozen with panic.

"Lexi?" says Lucas.

No answer. She's terrified, dark eyes dilated and locked on to the screen.

Lucas turns to check the monitor, but the red flashes

have stopped. Onscreen, Ralph the Mighty kneels, unmoving, waiting for the game to log off. Suddenly a harsh shriek seems to split the speakers. Lucas and Lexi both jump with fear. Something is approaching with furious, wicked intensity.

Lucas shouts, *"Run!"*

(5)

SOMETHING OUT THERE

Stoneship Woods is scary. Legends of its depravity abound in Carrolton kid circles. Brown bark-spiders drop from branches, puncture your eyes, and then as you stumble blindly they crawl into your ears to lay eggs. Meanwhile, showers of East Asian brain-beetles latch onto your skull and start drilling for a snack. Basically, your head is insect food here. So nobody in Carrolton really *wants* to go into Stoneship Woods.

Anyway, you can't even penetrate the tree line without a Makita chain saw—unless you happen to know the secret Team Spy Gear route.

Jake and Cyril slink bravely (or stupidly) through the bushes that mark the perimeter of the woods. Jake pushes aside a low sapling and approaches a solid wall of twisted trunks and high woven branches.

"I still get the creeps in here," says Cyril, spinning to check his back a couple of times.

"It's unpleasant," admits Jake.

Cyril looks up quickly. "What's that?" he says.

Jake glances at Cyril. Then he looks up. "What?"

Cyril whispers, *"That buzzing!"*

Jake, who has known Cyril all of his sentient life, tries not to roll his eyes. He stops politely to listen. After a moment he says, "You know, I don't actually hear anything, although God knows I'm trying."

Cyril slowly swivels his head, looking from side to side. With wide eyes, he examines the high branches. Then he whips out a small Spy Scope and continues his search for Tiny Bits of Death. Jake shakes his head, watching this.

"It's gone," says Cyril finally.

"Perhaps we can proceed then," says Jake.

Cyril bends over, rubs his hair vigorously, and then examines the ground. After a few seconds of pawing through leaves, he looks at Jake. "Nothing," he says with relief. "Let's move on."

"Are you sure?" asks Jake.

"Come on, we don't have all day!" exclaims Cyril.

Jake nods, grinning.

Cyril tries to rub the sweat off his hands. "Jake, it never hurts to be cautious," he says.

Jake nods with a grim smile. Then he spots a slim,

leafless birch wedged in the tree line. An X has been carved subtly into a knot on its trunk. He says, "Ah, here it is."

Cyril helps Jake push, low on the trunk. The bottom of the birch tears loose from its stump and swivels backward. But its high branches, tightly interlocked with those of its neighbors, keep the birch from falling over. In fact, a close examination of the highest branches would reveal several coils of nylon cord securing them to neighboring branches as well. (Some of you may recognize the work of a small, acrobatic monkey-girl here.)

Jake and Cyril step through the opening.

On the other side, they put their shoulders into the marked tree trunk and shove it back into place.

Ten minutes later, Cyril sits in a leather captain's chair at a large console, punching buttons. A bank of monitors flickers to life. Our mop-haired super spy gazes at the main monitor, a huge flat panel display in the middle of the console.

Jake stands beside the chair. He holds the Omega Link, a sleek silver rectangle of buffed metal. It has no knobs, no buttons or keys, no discernible control switches, nothing but a small display screen seamlessly beveled into the slim casing. The only marking at all is the aforementioned Greek omega symbol etched lightly on the casing.

Jake stares at the screen.

"That's a comma there, all right," he says.

"See?"

Jake turns the Omega Link sideways. He stares some more. Then he shakes his head and puts the gadget down on the console desk.

He says, "Maybe it's not a comma. Maybe it's a flaw in the display."

"Maybe," says Cyril, still focusing on the console's central display screen.

Jake shrugs. "You're sure it beeped?"

"Yep."

"Well, I'm stumped," says Jake.

He glances around the amazing room. The console monitors, two on each side, can televise views from numerous Minicams mounted in familiar Carrolton locations, plus others mounted in remote, unfamiliar locations. The system even controls the feed from a satellite-mounted camera. Its telescopic lenses feature absolutely stunning powers of magnification.

Eerily, this abandoned equipment all works like new. It hums away with smug, state-of-the-art efficiency. Then Jake turns to gaze at the gleaming array of pristine spy gadgets lining a shelf on the opposite wall. Team Spy Gear used some of these gadgets to complete their first espionage caper in Book One, foiling a dastardly plot to bring down the Internet.

* * *

Suddenly, a beeping sound shocks both boys into silence.

Cyril and Jake stare at each other.

"*I'll get it!*" they shout in perfect unison.

Both boys dive for the device. Although it's hard to overstate the brotherly closeness between Jake Bixby and Cyril Wong, they *are* boys. One Immutable Law of Boys is that when something beeps, *you* must be the first boy to obtain and examine the device, even if everything else in the room breaks in the process.

After a few minutes of brutal struggle, Jake's natural athleticism wins out over Cyril's raw howling intensity, and the Bixby boy triumphantly holds up the Omega Link to examine its screen.

Jake stares at it for a second.

Then he says, "Huh?"

Cyril, bleeding profusely, looks over Jake's shoulder. Okay, actually he's not bleeding. But several chunks of his hair now lie like wounded animals on the floor and yeah, okay, maybe that's an exaggeration too, but he's definitely kind of tired.

Cyril says, "Wait! I know that!"

Jake hands over the device. "This?"

The screen reads: BEOWULF/GRENDEL

Cyril nods excitedly. "Yes, Beowulf is a computer file folder. I've seen it in the network archives."

"Thank goodness," says Jake, relieved. "I was afraid it might be a homework assignment."

Cyril hands the device back to Jake, leaps into the captain's chair, and starts typing furiously on the console keyboard. A network search engine quickly pulls up a folder icon labeled Beowulf.

"The archive has so many folders, I've never opened this one," says Cyril, clicking on it. The Beowulf folder opens, revealing dozens of MPEG video files listed in alphabetical order. Cyril scans down to the G listings and finds a series of three files named Grendel_1, Grendel_2, and Grendel_3.

"Son of a gun," says Jake. "There it is."

Cyril double-clicks on the first Grendel file. A grainy surveillance video plays. It's dark, but Jake can make out tall grasses and a thicket of trees. It looks like a clearing in a forest. "Does that look familiar to you?" he asks Cyril.

"Not really," says Cyril. "It could be any forest, anywhere."

"Look!"

A dark figure rises slowly like a shadow from the tall grass. But before it fully emerges, the video file ends. The boys exchange a look, and then Cyril quickly clicks open Grendel_2. As the file flickers to life onscreen, Cyril gasps.

"Holy goats!" says Jake. "*That* doesn't look human."

Cyril can't even speak.

The dark figure turns sideways very, very slowly. Its head bobs, as if sniffing. From the side, the figure's head looks elongated, tapered to a snout. The lighting is poor, revealing no features. But the silhouette indicates a creature (for clearly it is not human) on four legs. The quadruped is large and lean. Suddenly it turns toward the camera. Red eyes gleam. Then its head jerks up, eyes skyward.

The beast slowly rises on its hind legs. Then the video ends.

Again the boys exchange a look. Then Cyril gazes down at the third file in the Grendel series.

"Do it," says Jake.

Cyril swallows and clicks.

The video window opens onscreen. The creature appears to be agitated now, standing on its hind legs. Its forelegs are short but powerful looking, tipped by visible claws. They strike out at the sky. All around, the foliage roils as if blown by a thunderstorm. Transfixed, Jake and Cyril watch, mouths open. The lean beast's eyes widen with blood-red fear.

Suddenly a cone of blinding reddish light bursts from the sky.

The creature is illuminated, but the light is too bright for the camera lens. The screen is awash in pure white for five, ten, fifteen seconds. The intensity forces both boys to squint. They can see nothing!

Finally the light disappears, switched off as suddenly as it came.

When the Minicam lens finally readjusts to darkness,

the beast is gone. The weeds still shudder wildly, but then their dark gyrations slowly cease. After a few more seconds, the clearing is as still as death—as if nothing at all had happened.

Jake and Cyril both exhale at the same time.

All of a sudden a pleasant female voice says: "Sensor three! Sensor three! Sensor three!"

6

MORE ODD THINGS

Mr. Latimer's Toyota idles in the passenger drop-off circle at Carlos Santana Middle School. Today is Saturday, so school is not in session. Mr. Latimer plugs a travel razor into his car's AC power outlet. Using the rearview mirror, he starts shaving.

Nearby, boys wander around the school grounds picking up litter. One of them, Nathan Fossil, notices Mr. Latimer and waves.

"Hey Mr. Latimer!" he calls.

"Hey there, Nathan," calls Mr. Latimer. "What are you doing?"

"Cleaning stuff," says Nathan.

"Why?"

Confused, Nathan looks around. He shrugs.

Another boy, Fletcher Norris, staggers toward the car. He says, "Hey, I got a new mountain bike."

Mr. Latimer says, "Good, Fletcher! Why aren't you out riding it?"

"I have to clean."

"Why?"

"I can't seem to articulate a reason," says Fletcher.

Fletcher looks over at Nathan, who shrugs. Both boys look at Mr. Latimer. They shrug.

"Interesting," says Mr. Latimer. He holds up his razor. "Well, boys, I've got to finish shaving. Back to your work!"

"It's not work!" reply Fletcher and Nathan, almost desperately.

Mr. Latimer looks at them for a second, then waves good-bye to the boys, who eagerly return to their task. He notices several girls on their hands and knees near the school entrance. They appear to be re-grouting the tile by the front door. Then he notices two men hailing him from across the grounds. He waves back. The two men, Mr. Rood and another Carrolton neighbor known as Dr. Tim, approach the car.

Mr. Rood leans down and solemnly shakes Mr. Latimer's hand. With more than a hint of sadness, he says, "Well, Bob, I think we've finally figured out how to get you to the Expressway."

"Okay," says Mr. Latimer. He turns off his razor and pulls out a small pad and pen.

Mr. Rood is an engineer who lives on Primrose Court, one of Mr. Latimer's favorite cul de sacs. Dr. Tim is the local fanatic. A former scientist with the National Center for Atmospheric Research, he got so obsessed with the widespread use of lawn poisons that he quit his job to start a lawn care service. Now he terrorizes neighbors who aren't organic. Dr. Tim's favorite tactic is to shriek through his huge white mustache while waving a Bolivian machete.

Mr. Rood tries to talk but chokes up. He defers to Dr. Tim, who nods and points down the street. *"Bob!"* shouts Dr. Tim. "I want you to head *straight* down Willow here!" He jabs his thumb sideways. "When you hit Ridgeview Drive, go right! Got it?"

"Got it," says Mr. Latimer, scribbling.

Dr. Tim falters. He tries to get his bearings. He looks up at the sun, then pulls out a compass and faces various directions. After a few minutes of this, Mr. Rood manages to speak again.

"Okay, so Bob, follow Ridgeview Drive past Ridgeview Court and Ridgeview Circle," says Mr. Rood. "Continue east. After you cross Willow again, you enter the West End traffic circle."

Now Dr. Tim consults a handheld GPS device. He taps in a few calculations, then jumps back in. "Bob, veer off the

West End circle at the second exit, which puts you onto Happer Comet Boulevard," says Dr. Tim. "It's a four-lane street, so get to the far right *immediately*, do you hear me? *Immediately!* Then turn right at the light, which is Wright."

"Wright?"

"Right. It's Wright."

"I go right?"

"Right."

Now Mr. Rood leans in.

"Continue along Wright just a block, then hang a left onto Willow. If you go too far here, Bob, you end up back on Ridgeview. Stay on Willow until you cross Ridgeview again. Got it?"

Mr. Latimer shakes a cramp out of his writing hand and continues. "Yes. Go ahead."

Dr. Tim gives him a sober, sad look. "Now, Bob, this is where it gets tricky."

"Okay."

"Stay on Willow as it curves left. When you hit Ridgeview again, go left, then take the very first right onto Willow. And Willow funnels you directly onto the Expressway, heading north." Dr. Tim looks down at the sidewalk. "I think."

"Is there a south entrance?"

"No! You can't go south."

"Anywhere?"

"*No!*"

Mr. Latimer nods grimly. So this is it, finally. He starts up his Toyota. With great feeling, he reaches out his window and warmly shakes hands with the two men. He swallows hard, then he drives off. Dr. Tim and Mr. Rood watch him go. They gaze sadly down the street after their good friend and neighbor of the past three years.

Ten minutes later Mr. Latimer pulls up behind them from the opposite direction.

At this point we have to ask: *Why can't Mr. Latimer find his way out of Carrolton?*

One theory is that Mr. Latimer secretly doesn't *want* to leave Carrolton, ever, because the people are friendly, the food is good, and everybody has nice dogs that don't bite or chase. Yes, I believe we referred to that line of thought earlier.

Another widely held theory is that Mr. Latimer's exit would mess up the book's plot, so the evil, greedy bean counters at Simon & Schuster make him stay against his will.

Plausible as that may seem, the truth here is that Mr. Latimer has a good reason for getting off track. He has indeed grown fond of the people in this happy community, so he's becoming concerned about odd things he keeps seeing.

For example, as he tried to follow his neighbors' directions through Carrolton, Mr. Latimer passed Stoneship

Woods. There, on Ridgeview Drive, he saw an unfamiliar car parked near the woods edge: a black BMW with U.S. Government license plates.

As Mr. Latimer trolled slowly past, he saw a huge dark figure melt into the trees.

The glimpse was brief. But Mr. Latimer could not deny what he saw in the man's hands: a heavy-duty set of wire cutters.

If indeed it *was* a man.

7

THROUGH THE EYES
OF THE BEAST

Jake and Cyril lock eyes, listening to the electronic voice: "Sensor three! Sensor three! Sensor three!" With the GRENDEL video image of a red-eyed beast fresh in mind, Jake feels an electric jolt of fear run up his spine. And if Jake is afraid, you can bet that Cyril is on the verge of organ failure.

"Sensor three," croaks Cyril. "Something's moving on the south perimeter."

"Are you sure?" says Jake.

Cyril lunges for a nearby metal case labeled SPY TRACKER SYSTEM, which emits the warning voice. He quickly flips open the lid, revealing a map of the warehouse and surrounding area. This map is hand-sketched on a green eight-by-eight grid. Black dots on the map mark the locations of three motion-sensor pods placed around the perimeter of the warehouse yard. Cyril looks at the map.

"Yes, I'm sure," he whispers.

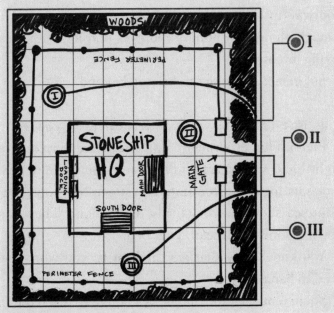

Cyril and Jake exchange a look.

"Lucas and Lexi, maybe?" suggests Cyril, his voice cracking.

Jake shakes his head. "They know better," he says quickly. "They know they'd trip the alarm. They wouldn't try a southern approach unless . . ."

"Unless it was an emergency," whispers Cyril.

Jake nods grimly.

"So if it's them, it's bad," says Cyril. "And if it *isn't* them . . ."

"It's bad," finishes Jake.

Jake rushes to the plate-glass window overlooking the warehouse floor below. He stares down at an open cargo doorway in the south wall. His imagination serves up a quick glimpse of hungry red eyes burning with meat-loving intensity.

But in fact, nothing can be seen beyond.

Kids, isn't it amazing what raw fear can make you see?

Here's a fun experiment: Tonight in bed, turn off your night-light so it's really dark, and think really scary thoughts for about ten minutes. Suggestion: Imagine if giant sea squids were actually amphibious. Then hang down to look underneath your bed.

You know, now that we think of it, you won't even need to hang down.

Squid tentacles are quite long enough to reach the top of the bed, slap their slimy sucker cups on your back, and pull you down like a wriggling fish. As I understand it, squids like to feed slowly. They insert you feet first between their tusks. Your head is the last thing that goes down the slobbery mouth canal. That way, you can watch the rest of yourself being eaten alive.

Isn't that nice?

And don't try to hide under the covers. It won't work. Squids aren't stupid.

* * *

"Cyril, let's play it safe," shouts Jake. "I think we need a lockdown!"

Cyril immediately punches a series of buttons on the console.

"Roger, intruder in the yard," he says with the grim inflection of a NASA mission control specialist in Houston. "Initiating lockdown procedures. Repeat, all systems are *go* for lockdown."

"And try to contact Lucas on the Spy Link," adds Jake, eyeing the cargo door nervously.

"Will do," says Cyril, punching another button. He leans to a microphone on the console. "Calling Lima Bravo, do you read me, over? Lima Bravo, Lima Bravo, please report, do you read me, over?"

"I'm heading down," says Jake, heading for the floor hatch. "Let's check all exits."

Cyril gulps. "Interesting idea," he says.

Slowly, very slowly, the south cargo door closes as the boys scramble down to the warehouse floor.

The last few minutes have been quite interesting for Lucas Bixby.

At the very moment that Cyril yells his call sign ("Lima Bravo"), Lucas is running through Stoneship Woods. But he doesn't hear Cyril, because he has jammed the headset of his hands-free Spy Link Communicator in a pocket. Why? Because hostile tree branches keep ripping it off his ear, that's why. Yes, Lucas runs. He runs wildly, in fact. He runs like a deranged marsupial. As you well know, this is the wildest, most insane type of run.

Lucas runs like this for good reason.

Something big is chasing him.

Is it a squid?

Let's read on and find out!

But first, let's back up a few minutes. About twenty ought to do it. Back, back to just after the last time we saw Lucas and Lexi playing M3.

It's a late October afternoon and, since daylight saving time ended last Sunday, darkness comes earlier. And check out that sky, will you? Slate gray clouds dangle and whirl like angry ghost battalions advancing over the trees. Note: This always happens whenever you approach Stoneship Woods.

Now look: Lucas and Lexi are backing away from the edge of Stoneship Woods. Are they afraid of something? The two walk backward up the street. Lexi shrugs. Lucas turns to Lexi and says, "?yako leef uoy *erus* uoy erA"

Wait a minute!

You're still backing up in time! Stop!

Go *forward* now, for gosh sakes!

Okay, that's better. Now Lucas and Lexi are walking forward down the street, approaching the edge of Stoneship Woods.

Lucas turns to Lexi and says, "Are you *sure* you feel okay?"

Lexi just shrugs.

Lucas nods, watching his pal closely. As they approach the woods, Lexi starts wringing her hands—a nervous gesture he's never seen her make before.

"Something weird is happening to you," says Lucas. "That game is messing you up, man."

"What game?" asks Lexi.

Lucas stares at her. Lexi's eyes look glazed, almost oily.

"Dude, didn't you see those flashing red lights?" asks Lucas.

"No."

Lexi suddenly stops. She looks up and down the tree line.

Lucas glances at the woods, then back at Lexi. He says, "What's wrong?"

Lexi takes a deep breath and says, "Something's in there."

"Yes!" says Lucas, trying desperately to be patient, as patience is not his strong suit. He speaks slowly. "The *warehouse* is in there. You know, like, our headquarters? And Jake and Cyril are in there too. Like, right now. Waiting for us." His words get faster. "And also, also, like, like the Omega Link is in there, and it's beeping. It has a comma on it or something. A comma! Do you understand?" Lucas loses all semblance of calm and starts hopping straight up and down. "The Omega Link is beeping! *It's calling us! It's calling us!*"

This actually seems to work. Lexi looks at Lucas, and a glimmer of the old fearless Lexi is in her chocolate eyes. She nods and sighs out some breath, and then the two friends proceed through the copse of scrub pines at the edge of the forest and—say, that phrase sounds familiar, doesn't it? Hmmm. Well, anyway, they plunge deeper into the forest. As they push forward, tree limbs snapping and popping, Lucas has a weird feeling. Up ahead, he sees a rocky outcropping in a patch of brush. Steam rises from a dark cleft in the rock.

"Whoa!" says Lucas, pointing.

And then it hits him. Has it hit *you* yet?

Here, let me give you another clue:

Lexi is frozen, motionless. Her eyes are wide. They look like wet glass. Then Lucas notices Lexi's hands. They're trembling.

Okay, got it yet? See, I just copied the previous paragraph directly from Chapter 4 and pasted it in here, word for word. And it continues.

Lucas stares at the cave.

"Yikes," he says. "Are those . . . *red eyes* in there?"

The two kids stare warily at the cave. Inside, red eyes blink, twice.

That's right. This very real location also appears in M3—in a *game*, the very game that Lexi and Lucas were playing just minutes ago in Chapter 4. Same trees, same geography. Same dark steaming rock cleft.

Same red eyes.

But then something freaky happens: *The camera moves!*

Kids, I'll need your help for this.

You see, in a book, the "camera" is actually inside the reader's mind, which is what's cool about books and should make you feel important.

Anyway, the camera view now moves inside the head of a creature in the trees, not far from Lucas and Lexi. Through the miracle of this modern literary device, *you* become the creature. You now see with the eyes of the beast! Look directly at our two Team Spy Gear kids through the reddish tint of the brute's eyes.

Good.

Now start grunting.

Louder!

Excellent. Now shriek.

Do it again, really loud, right now!

This second shriek has to be loud enough to scare the bejabbers out of anybody who is unfortunate enough to be anywhere nearby. If you're in a public place like a library or bookstore, you want to shriek loud enough so that babies start crying.

Well done!

That was just a test, actually. The creature in the book doesn't shriek.

The grunting hairy "beast" in the book just stares quietly

through the foliage at Lucas. It grunts again and nods, as if recognizing the younger Bixby brother. Then it makes the same grunting nod of recognition at Lexi. Don't you wish the beast was carrying a mirror, so you could gaze at your reflection right now and see exactly what you look like?[5]

Wow, all this high-tech camera manipulation is *really* slowing down the action, isn't it?

Okay, let's fix that right now.

Through your reddish haze of vision, you see Lexi suddenly point at you.

She shrieks. This is a real shriek.

Lucas squints in terror at the branches that hide your position.

Lexi turns and runs.

Lucas follows her, glancing over his shoulder at your location in sheer fright.

You push forward through the bushes and follow them, tracking the children.

You grunt and gasp and snort. Hair hangs in your eyes. You hear the *clomp clomp clomp* of your heavy feet as you run. You hear the sizzle of acidic drool as it drips from your mouth and hits the ground, burning a hideous smoking trail in the leaves as you run, or maybe not, maybe no drool, maybe that's just extra, okay, but I love the sound of it, don't you? You hear other curious sounds too. For one, a cell phone snapping open. Buttons pressed: *Beep beep beep!* The shocking,

5. Unfortunately, most beasts don't carry mirrors, although amazingly enough, some do.

60

gruesome hiss of a dial-up connection being made.

Wait a minute.

What kind of monster *are* you, anyway?

Okay, hop back out of the monster's head now. It's uncomfortable, and I really don't like all that hair, do you? Up ahead, Lucas tries desperately to catch Lexi, whose terror has propelled her to Olympic levels of speed and agility.

Behind him, Lucas hears the heavy footfall and deep rasping of the large pursuer.

Lucas Bixby has a very vivid picture in his mind of this pursuer. Just minutes ago, back in Lexi's house, he watched Ralph the Mighty get torn into marbled meat chunks by a dark beast of terrifying strength and ferocity. Its carnivorous red eyes burned an imprint into the fear circuitry of Lucas's brain. Now Lucas is pretty sure that an actual version of this very creature is chasing him. As a result, he's running faster than quantum physics.

Yet he's still not fast enough to catch The Amazing Lexi.

Lucas glimpses his panic-stricken friend up ahead.

It sort of looks like she's flying.

Heaving vapor like a large bulldozer, only smaller, Lucas bursts into a grassy clearing, maybe fifty feet in diameter—a totally unfamiliar location. On the meadow's opposite side is an impenetrable clump of birch trees, whitish trunks and low branches linked like an ogre's white picket fence. Lucas sees Lexi suddenly veer right and bound like a mad kangaroo up into the lowest branches of a huge cottonwood tree towering over the birch clump. She scrambles through the dead leaves of an opening high in the ancient tree and disappears.

Lucas hears gasps. Is his pal sobbing?

A strange protective instinct overcomes our young Bixby. He spots a small worn path in the bushes to the left of the birch clump—that is, the opposite side from where Lexi disappeared. He heads toward it but stops before entering the path.

He turns abruptly to face his pursuer.

"Hey!" he shouts. "Hey hey! Ugly boy! Over here! This way, Quasimodo!"

He makes a gesture back toward the trees where Heavy Footsteps of Pursuit approach the clearing.

To be perfectly honest . . . well, it's not a very nice gesture.

The red eyes of the beast see Lucas's gesture. They watch as Lucas then turns and dashes into the trees.

The creature steps out into the clearing.

It takes a step toward where Lucas just disappeared. But then it hears a cracking, crunching sound in the huge cottonwood tree to its right, and the scream of a girl. The scream ends abruptly.

Without a thought, it turns toward the cottonwood and follows Lexi's scream.

8

RETURN OF THE NEMESIS

Lucas hears the scream too. He skids to a halt and looks around, panting.

He has no idea where he's at.

Following his first instinct, he turns toward the scream and starts shouting.

"Lexi!" he yells. "Lexi!"

No answer.

Lucas dives into the brush and briars, thrashing toward the scream. But the nasty Stoneship shrubbery reaches out to shove him left, then right. Creeper vines grab his ankles and trip him up. Lucas swings and kicks wildly, trying to fight through. But after a few seconds, he loses his bearings.

He stops to listen. Not a sound now.

"Lexi!" he calls.

No reply. And no sound of the monster behind him either.

Lucas grits his teeth tightly. Why didn't the beast follow him? A deep pang of guilt suddenly hits him like a lacrosse stick in the gut. If there's one thing a Bixby is, it's this: deeply, fiercely loyal. Lucas feels a sudden wave of anger and sickness. Did his split-second decision to lure the pursuer backfire? *I should have followed Lexi,* he thinks desperately. *I'm a flipping idiot!* If he'd just stayed between Lexi and the Slorg, the red-eyed beast would be munching on *him* now instead of on his best pal. And you know what? That would be just fine with Lucas Bixby, just fine.

Wait! Who said "Slorg"?

Oh, right. It was me.

So you're probably asking, "What's a Slorg?" As everyone who plays M3 knows, the Slorg (there is only one) is the most fearsome red-eyed carnivore in all of continental Banglandia, the land where Westhaven was founded.

Apparently that high honor wasn't good enough for the beast, since it appears to be expanding its operations into the real world now.

Lucas spins around, trying to regain his bearings. Some are on the ground. Other bearings are in Bob Bolby's pocket about twenty miles away, in a Subway just outside

Norfolk. Who's Bob Bolby? We don't know. So forget the bearings. In frustration, Lucas just starts running.

He bursts through an elderberry hedge and slams into a security fence. Boy, that looks painful.

And that brings us twenty minutes forward, right back to the present.

As you probably guessed, the security fence that Lucas Bixby just encountered nose first lines the southern perimeter of the Stoneship warehouse yard. A Spy Tracker motion-sensor pod sits on a nearby rock; this pod sensed his movement, triggering the alarm inside the Stoneship control room.

Lucas, holding his mashed nose, staggers along the security fence.

The main entrance gate, he knows, is open. But as he stumbles through low evergreen limbs, he comes to a small section of fence that looks torn open. Lucas ducks through the opening. Up ahead, he sees the warehouse's south cargo door slowly sliding shut. He bursts into a full sprint as the door drops, then makes a diving baseball slide under the door just before it clangs shut. *Safe!*

On the other side, Lucas looks up. Jake and Cyril stand there, looking down at him.

"*Blood!*" shrieks Cyril.

Jake immediately grabs the slumping Cyril, who has

been known to faint at the sight of human fluids. Lucas holds out the hand that covers his nose. Yep, it's covered with blood. Ouch!

"I ran into the fence," says Lucas quickly. "Lexi's in trouble!"

Jake senses a desperate urgency in his little brother's voice. He lets go of Cyril, who drops to the floor like a sack of rubber chickens.

"What kind of trouble?" asks Jake.

"Something's out there," gasps Lucas, still trying to catch his breath.

"What is it?"

"Something bad."

"Did you see it?"

Lucas nods yes, but says, "No."

This contradictory response may seem odd, but in fact it's completely understandable. Lucas has not actually seen anything but the red glow of eyes. His amygdala, however—an almond-shaped mass of gray matter in the lateral ventricle of his brain, sometimes called the brain's Fear Center—has helped Lucas see more. His Fear Center sees a Slorg, right now.

Lucas says, "I heard a scream." He looks at his brother. Suddenly, tears fill his eyes.

Wow, okay, that's all Jake needs to see. His own lingering fears dissolve to blank inconsequential nothingness. He grabs his little brother and gently lifts him to his feet.

He yanks a Spy Link headset out of his pocket, slides it over his ear, and plugs its cord into the walkie-talkie unit clipped on his belt. Then he turns and runs directly to the south cargo door.

"Let's go!" he shouts back. "Cyril! Get this door back open!"

Cyril hears the no-nonsense tone in Jake's voice and immediately snaps out of his swoon.

"Aye, aye, sir!" says Cyril, scrambling to his feet with a snappy salute. He hustles to the recessed ladder rungs on the wall, clambers back up to the control room, and dives into the captain's chair at the command console, punching at buttons before his butt even hits the black leather.

The cargo door slides open.

Jake scoots under and bursts into the yard. Lucas, holding his bloody nose, follows Jake.

Cyril punches more buttons and taps in a few commands on the console keyboard. New camera angles flicker to life on the bank of monitors above the console. The screens show various views of the yard and forest surrounding the Stoneship warehouse.

"Okay, team, I've got all the local surveillance feeds cued up," says Cyril into the console mike. "Shall we go to Eye-Link voiceless com?"

No time! shouts Lucas breathlessly. His voice emanates from the console speakers.

Cyril nods and says, "Roger that. Stay with Spy Link vox com." He quickly scans the monitors. "Guys, I don't see anything. No movement."

Outside now, Jake dashes toward the south perimeter fence. "Where do we start, bro?" he asks Lucas.

Lucas points to the small opening ripped in the fence. "There," he says.

Jake frowns as he pulls himself carefully through the jagged hole. He says, "Dude, I don't recall seeing this before."

Lucas follows, too concerned about Lexi to focus much on the obvious security breach. His nosebleed has let up, but his face is still smeared with blood and tears. He bursts past Jake and dashes into the forest, crashing through bushes as he tries to retrace the route back to the cottonwood clearing where he and Lexi split up.

"Cyril, we need overhead," says Jake, ducking branches as he runs after his brother. "I have no clue where we are or where we're going."

Roger, going to satellite camera on main monitor now, says Cyril's voice in their earpieces. He sounds a little uneasy about this prospect.

"It won't help," huffs Lucas. "They're in the deep forest."

"Well, it can't hurt," says Jake.

* * *

Cyril *really* dislikes accessing the satellite spy-cam available via the Stoneship command console. Yes, its telescopic lens features unbelievably stunning powers of resolution. And sure, it's kind of fun to look down and zoom in on the backyard antics of mean girls you hate. But Cyril can't help but believe that tapping into a multi-million-dollar geostationary satellite array is a sure way to attract unwanted attention from someone big and scary and probably dressed in black.

At Cyril's insistence, the boys had agreed to limit sat-cam use to emergency situations only. And although *this* situation certainly qualifies as a good candidate, it still makes Cyril very, very nervous to call up the aerial view of Carrolton.

Cyril grabs the mouse, moves the onscreen pointer over Stoneship Woods, and clicks the left mouse button. The view zooms closer. He spots the warehouse, a white square from above, and keeps left-clicking on it until it expands to fill half the screen. Then he right-clicks and drags the view over the south perimeter area. Cyril has to shake his head at the remarkable simplicity of this sat-cam control interface.

"I don't see you," he says into the console mike.

He hears panting. Then he hears Jake's voice: I think we're lost. More panting. Then: Yes, yes, confirmed. We're lost.

"That didn't take long," remarks Cyril.

Wait! Lucas, is that—?

Oh, no! cries Lucas.

"What's wrong, guys?" says Cyril tensely. "What is it?"

We're back where we started! says Jake. At the dang perimeter fence.

Cyril turns to look at one of the smaller side monitors, a view of the south yard. Sure enough, there stand Jake and Lucas in the bushes, not far from a nasty-looking hole in the chain-link security fence.

Cyril! calls Lucas. He sounds terrible. He says, Scan around and see if you can find an open area just south of the security fence. Like, a little meadow. Just grass. And you should see a huge honking cottonwood tree at one end.

"Roger that," says Cyril. "Scanning now."

He drags the sat-cam view around. Within seconds he finds the enormous cottonwood and the clearing.

"Bingo on that, Lima Bravo," he says.

Can you guide us to it? asks Lucas. Give us directions from the fence.

"Roger," says Cyril. "Get out your compasses, boys."

Cyril's directions are right on the money. After all, the kid loves maps. In games, in books, if it has a map, Cyril Wong can't stop exploring it. He once spent forty-eight straight sleepless hours poring over the Third Day of the

Battle of Gettysburg in a Civil War battlefield map book. Or maybe it was forty-eight minutes. It was a long time. Look, Cyril loves maps. Got it? Okay, good, now maybe we can move on.

As the Bixbys hustle across the clearing toward the cottonwood tree, Jake gets the full scoop from Lucas on Lexi's odd behavior while playing M3.

"Dude, that game is seriously twisting her braids," says Lucas, jogging through the high meadow grasses. "The minute the Slorg burst out of its den, she totally screamed and, like, covered up her eyes! Her avatar guy, Ralph the Mighty, got totally mauled. She didn't even fight back."

Jake squints at his brother. "Wait. *Lexi* didn't fight back?"

Lucas nods. "See? It's nuts."

"And this actual cave opening you found in the woods," says Jake. "You're saying it resembles the one in the game, in M3?"

Lucas stops and peers up into the cottonwood's high branches. "No," he says. "It didn't *resemble* it." He looks at Jake. "It was the *same cave*." He nods again with absolute certainty. "And I mean *exactly* the same."

"You're sure?"

"Yes."

"The cave in M3 and the real cave in the woods are the same?"

"Straight word, straight up, dude."

I can't tell you how much that creeps me out, says Cyril's voice in their ears.

Jake says, "Seems like there's more to M3 than just a game."

Way, says Cyril. There's been a lot of highly disturbing behavior at school ever since the game was released two weeks ago. Kids behaving, helping, that sort of nonsense. It's ape, I tell you.

"Lexi!" shouts Lucas. "Yo! Lexi, man!" He grabs a branch and tries to swing himself up to the opening, which is about ten feet up the cottonwood's trunk. "Hey, give me a boost here, Jake."

Jake gets under his brother and hefts him upward. Lucas scrambles from limb to limb, then swings into the gap in the branches, disappearing from sight.

"Cyril, what's the word?" asks Jake, glancing around the clearing.

Nothing marked, reports Cyril. Nothing on local spy-cams, nothing on satellite overhead.

"What you got in there, bro?" he calls to Lucas.

After a short pause, he hears crunching leaves and snapping twigs. Then, suddenly, Lucas pops his head through the gap. He looks sick.

"She fell," he says.

"What? How do you know?"

"There's a freshly broken branch up high. Underneath

that, more branches are broken." Agitated, Lucas hangs from a limb and drops next to Jake. "But she's gone. She's not there. The Slorg got her!"

Jake seizes his brother's arm. "Lucas, there's no such thing as a Slorg."

Suddenly Cyril's voice crackles in their ears. He says, **Lucas, my man. A question.**

Lucas, who looks on the verge of panic, takes a deep breath. "Yeah?"

Did she have her tracker?

Lucas's eyes suddenly grow so big they look like painted eggs. "Holy snow geese!" he shouts. He immediately rips open a Velcro pocket in his baggy cargo pants and pulls out a hand-sized gadget with the words AGENT TRACKER etched on it. Across its front, LED lights are arrayed in three arcs. Lucas activates this seeker module; the arc lights start flashing blue for "Cold." He holds the unit out in front of him and rotates slowly. He turns to the right and takes a few steps; the arc lights now flash yellow for "Getting Warmer."

"*Yes!*" yells Lucas.

"What the monkey is that?" asks Jake.

"Handheld tracking device," says Lucas. "Indicates direction and distance!"

"Direction and distance to what?"

To the tracking bug in Lexi's pocket, you clueless goat,

says Cyril. Don't you listen to your own brother's Gadget Utilization Seminars? Gosh, we've only had about seven of them since discovering the warehouse.

"Actually, no," says Jake, grinning for the first time in a while. "So this Agent Tracker will lead us right to Lexi? Hey, wait for me, dude!"

Lucas is already running across the clearing.

You know, guys, says Cyril, it's getting dangerously close to what many people would consider "night."

Jake glances upward. The sky is indeed darkening rapidly. "Yeah," he says, wading through the meadow grass after Lucas. "Lucas! It's getting dark."

Up ahead, Lucas stops. Still staring at the arc lights on the tracking module, he rips open another Velcro pants pocket and pulls out a Spy Night Scope. He tosses the sleek night-vision binoculars to Jake. Then he pulls a smaller gadget—a mini night-vision lens called a Nightspyer—out of another pocket. He flicks on the gadget's red LED beam, peeks through the scope to scout ahead, and then nods and continues moving forward, still following the flashing Agent Tracker's directional bearings.

"Man, is there anything you *don't* have in your pants?" asks Jake in amazement. Then, after a pause, he says, "Don't answer that."

"This way!" shouts Lucas.

* * *

74

The Bixby boys stumble through a patch of fiddlehead ferns onto a moss-covered path. Lucas wields the tracker module with almost insane intensity.

"We're getting close!" he hisses, staring at the gadget as he walks.

"It's getting darker," says Jake with concern.

You know, that happens almost every night, says Cyril's voice in the Bixbys' earpieces.

All of a sudden Lucas stops dead in his tracks. He stops so abruptly that Jake runs into his back.

"Whoa!"

Jake follows his brother's gaze. Up ahead is a rocky outcropping. Steam rises from a cleft, barely visible in the fading light.

In the brush just below the rocks stands a large, hulking figure.

It turns slowly to face the Bixbys. Two red eyes glow dimly in the dusk.

"*Jake!*" says Lucas. But he can speak no more.

Jake tries to answer but cannot.

The red eyes remain motionless for a second. Then, slowly, they begin to approach.

Yo, what's the up-front, dudes? calls Cyril brightly over the Spy Link. **What's going on? Are you there? Hello? Hello? Yo, Bixbys!**

Jake yanks the Spy Link headset from his ear and lets it dangle. Then he instinctively slides in front of Lucas and drops into a defensive crouch. But as the red eyes advance, a dim outline of the creature becomes visible against the dusky sky. It is a big-headed, wild-haired beast, yes.

And here's something really disturbing.

It carries a small, limp, long-haired corpse in its arms.

The monster crouches to place its kill on the ground and hunkers down to feed. The slavering fiend reaches a huge paw up to its face, presumably to wipe drool from its fangs, or beak, or whatever.

Then slowly, it flips its red eyes upward.

"Keep this kid out of trees, will you?" says the monster.

"My ankle hurts," says the corpse.

The monster nods and looks at the Bixbys. "You dudes got any ibuprofen?"

9

BLACK BIRD

Hey, that voice sounds familiar.

In the stunned silence that follows the monster's request for pain medication, Lucas Bixby recovers his wits long enough to whip out his XP-4 Spy Pen. He shines its mini-flashlight at the familiar voice.

Sure enough, the bright light reveals a familiar visage, too.

Lucas and Jake gasp at the same time: *"Marco!"*

Tangled dreadlocks hang in the monster's face. On his forehead, flipped upward, nestles a pair of infrared night-vision goggles. Still crouching, Marco holds up a hand to block the glare.

Lucas lowers the light beam. Now it shines on the tiny body at Marco's feet.

"Yo," says Lexi, waving feebly.

Then Marco says, *"Kill that light!* You want them to see us?"

This is actually the second time the Bixbys have mistaken Marco for a monster. And, as you may (or may not) have guessed by now, the red-eyed "Beast-Cam" we were looking through back in Chapter 7 was actually the goggled eyes of Marco.

Spy Gear fans will of course remember Marco as the scruffy überhacker who coordinated a dastardly attack on the Internet in Book One of this Spy Gear Adventure series, available in a bookstore near you except for the stupid bookstores that don't have it. Fortunately, Marco's sly cyberassault was foiled by our heroes. That, of course, was back in Book One of this Spy Gear Adventure series, available in a bookstore near you, and by the way, it's always a good idea to purchase three or four copies, just in case.

Anyway, the last time the Bixby boys saw Marco, he was being hauled off in shackles by mysterious black-suited men in a convoy of black cars.

Just before that, his last words to Jake were as follows: "I'll get you, Bixby. If it's the last thing I do."

Lucas puts his hand over the mini-light to dim it, but he doesn't turn it off. The ghostly, reddish illumination makes Marco look even scarier as he rises slowly from his crouch.

"I think you know why I'm here," says Marco ominously, looking at Jake.

Jake nods tensely. "Revenge," he says.

"Exactly," says Marco.

Yo, homeys, can I get a report here? shouts Cyril via the Spy Link.

"Shut *up*, Cyril!" says Lucas.

Marco looks around, then turns back to Lucas, grimly amused. "Cyril, eh?" he says.

Lucas notes the smirk and says, "I'm not talking to you. I'm talking to someone else."

Marco nods. "Okay," he says.

Dude, what's the 411? shouts Cyril.

"Cyril, you goat!" says Lucas with exasperation, putting a finger to his Spy Link earpiece. "We have a *Code Yellow* here!"

Marco says, "I had an invisible friend when I was little too."

Down on the ground, Lexi snorts.

Marco glares down at her. "What are you laughing at?" he says.

"You!" says Lexi.

"Why?" roars Marco.

"Because you're funny!" yells Lexi.

Jake and Lucas exchange a look. Suddenly Marco reaches down toward Lexi. Lucas leaps forward and shines the mini-light at Marco's face. Blinded, Marco howls and staggers backward. As Lucas jabs the light outward, his hand accidentally hooks his Spy Gear headset, yanking it roughly off his ear.

Jake quickly hops over Lexi and plants himself between the prone girl and Marco.

"Leave her out of it!" shouts Jake.

"Out of what?" growls Marco, shielding his eyes.

Lucas yells, "Your hideous, bloodthirsty designs of vengeance!"

"Wow," says Marco, squinting at the brothers. "Really, could you guys, like, stop *shouting*?"

"Your business is with us, not her," says Jake, raising his fists.

"No, it isn't," says Marco.

"Yes, it is."

"No, it isn't."

"Yes, it is!"

"Guys, it isn't."

"Oh yeah?" says Lucas.

"Yeah."

"Really?" asks Jake. He drops his fists.

"Yes, really." Marco rubs his temples. "My God, you guys are loud."

"Well," says Lucas, looking perplexed, "if your evil revenge isn't with us, then who?"

"The dude who set me up," says Marco with sudden bitterness.

"You mean . . . Viper?" says Lucas.

Marco gives Lucas a wary look. He says, "How do you know about Viper?"

Lucas glances at Jake. Jake shrugs and makes a gesture that says, *Go ahead, tell him*. So Lucas says, "Well, we don't really *know* about Viper. We just saw his name. Signed to an e-mail. Uh, an e-mail on your computer. Back at your farmhouse. Right before, uh, you know . . ."

"Right before you trashed about eleven thousand dollars worth of my equipment," says Marco darkly.

"That was me," pipes up Lexi. She raises her hand. "I did it."

Marco glares down at her again. "You don't have to be so perky about it," he says.

"It was fun," says Lexi.

"I thought you were hurt," says Marco.

"I am. That's why you carried me so far, remember?"

"Then maybe you should, like, stop talking."

Gingerly, Lexi pushes herself to her feet. "I sprained my ankle."

"*Good!* Now shut up, will you?"

Lexi snorts again. She really seems to get a kick out of Marco.

* * *

At this point it behooves us to do another short recap of the first Spy Gear Adventure in Book One. Several weeks ago, Marco and a gang of rebel hackers nearly brought down the worldwide Internet. The attack, as noted earlier, was thwarted by Jake, Lucas, Cyril, and especially Lexi, who personally tore Marco's high-tech hacker's nest to shreds.

In the course of doing so, Lexi found part of an e-mail on the screen of Marco's computer—an e-mail signed by someone using the name "Viper." The note suggested that Viper was the mastermind of the Internet scheme, and it hinted at even bigger and perhaps darker plans afoot. Lexi had the good sense to snap a photo of the onscreen e-mail with her Spy Camera.

The e-mail photo sits in an impenetrable Spy Safecracker system back at the Stoneship command post. If you want to actually *read* the Viper's e-mail, you'll have to either crack the safe's entry code or else pick up Book One of the Spy Gear Adventure series, available without a doubt at a fine bookstore near you.

Speaking of the stoneship command post, maybe we should check in on Cyril, who is on the verge of insanity back at the console after hearing things like *Marco!* and *We have a Code Yellow here!* and distant howling and yelling and then no more response from the Bixby boys.

In fact, at this very moment, Cyril is digging in his pocket for his cell phone and screaming into the console microphone, "Jake! Lucas! Answer me! What's going on? Did he kill you? Are you maimed? *Jake!*"

No answer.

"I'm calling 911!" screams Cyril, digging in dozens of pants pockets. "I'm calling 911! I'm calling 911!" He rips open more Velcro. "Uh, just as soon as I find my cell phone." Cyril searches more pockets. He has about two or three hundred pockets, I believe, so this could take hours, or perhaps days.

Finally, over the console speakers, he hears Lucas say, Cyril! Chill!

"Why? What's wrong with Jake? Why doesn't he answer?"

Cyril hears a rustling sound over the speakers. Then, finally, Jake speaks.

Sorry, man. I took off my headset.

"Why?"

Because your voice was really loud and shrill and, you know, annoying.

"Okay," says Cyril, nodding. "Okay, that makes sense."

No offense, dude. I had to focus on the situation.

"Cool," says Cyril. "Whatever."

You won't believe this, Cyril, says Lucas. Marco's back! And he's like, well, uh, he's all, he's all . . .

Lucas hesitates.

"He's all what?" says Cyril. "What is he all?"

He's sort of on our side.

Cyril widens his eyes. "How could that be? I mean, we messed him up, big-time." He shakes his hair. "Dude, we got him *arrested*."

What can I say? says Jake. It's totally goats.

Suddenly, Cyril hears a beep. Then another. He turns to the sound.

It's the Omega Link!

"Field team, we're getting Omega input!" says Cyril quickly, grabbing the shiny device. He scans its display screen and says, "Roger that. We have input. I repeat, *we have Omega input*."

The sound of Lucas whooping loudly nearly blows the console speakers. Cyril turns down the volume a bit, then turns back to the Omega Link.

On its display screen, figures slowly appear one by one, as if being typed:

$$X I , \quad 1 - 2$$
$$X I , \quad 3 1 - 3 3$$

When the typing finally stops, Cyril grabs the console microphone and pulls it toward him.

Breathlessly, he says, "Guys, I have—"

What's that? says Jake suddenly. Do you hear that?

Where is it? says Lucas.

It's up there!

Where?

In the sky! See it?

Yes!

Cyril hears a low, rhythmic thumping sound coming through the speakers.

"What's that, guys?" he asks with grave alarm. "Guys?"

Get down! Get in the bushes!

Over here, dude!

Douse that light!

Marco! Help Lexi, will you?

Hurry! Hurry!

Get down!

Marco, Lexi, and the Bixbys hunker in the foliage, all eyes on the sky.

A black helicopter thrums almost silently above the rocky outcropping. After a few seconds, a powerful green-hued searchlight bursts brilliantly from the underside of the copter's black, beetle-like shell. Greenish light shines on the rugged crag of rock. It reveals a small cave opening. Vapor drifts from the mouth.

Lucas can't help it. Transfixed by the awesome obsidian aircraft, he slowly raises his head to see it more clearly.

"No!" says Marco. "Stay down!" He gives Lucas a fierce look. "They can see *everything*!"

Chastened, Lucas drops back down. Marco crouches with one hand on each of the younger kids' backs. Jake notices this and manages a slight smile. Then he taps Marco's shoulder.

"Who are they?" he asks quietly.

"It's *them*," says Marco.

"The guys who arrested you?"

"That would be my guess."

Jake stares up at the elegant black craft. "What are they looking for?"

"Something in that cave, obviously." Indeed, the brilliant green spotlight has not wandered yet from the cave mouth.

"Like what?" asks Lucas.

"You don't want to know."

"Why not?"

Marco glares at him. "Because you're a bunch of little kids."

After a few seconds, the dazzling searchlight switches off, and darkness returns. Jake looks around, realizing just *how* dark it is now. Night has almost fully fallen, even though its only 6:00 p.m. The sleek craft hovers: looking, looking. The whirling blades beat with a quiet whine, not the loud *chop chop chop* that Jake hears when traffic helicopters patrol the nearby Expressway.

Finally, after forever, the black craft rises slowly, pivots, and speeds away.

* * *

From his blue Toyota Avalon on Ridgeview Drive, Mr. Latimer watches the black airship drift slowly over Stoneship Woods. Then it swivels and darts with stunning speed into the horizon's indigo gloom.

The craft disappears in mere seconds. Wow!

Mr. Latimer blinks. Did he really see that?

Suddenly he detects movement in the trees.

Look! The same large, dark figure Mr. Latimer saw entering the woods earlier now emerges, returning to the black BMW—the one with U.S. Government license plates parked at the forest's edge on Ridgeview Drive, remember? Dressed in a black overcoat or cloak, with a black hat pulled low over the face, the ominous intruder slinks through the high grasses beside the road.

Wait.

Why is he going *that* way?

Doesn't he know about—?

Oops.

Mr. Latimer watches with interest as the dark figure trips and falls into Blackwater Creek. After splashing and flailing around for a few seconds, the mysterious dark intruder stumbles angrily out of the streambed and staggers directly toward his car.

Gee, thinks Mr. Latimer. *The guy must not be familiar with the area.*

For example, the intruder doesn't seem to be aware of the low split-log railing hidden by high grasses along the roadside.

Ouch!

The collision itself looks painful enough. But wow, that full-body flip afterward—that has to hurt pretty badly.

Mr. Latimer watches the shadowy intruder crawl to its BMW, dragging one leg and holding its face.

POWWOW AT HQ

The decision to invite Marco to Team Spy Gear's HQ is a no-brainer. Hey, it's dark, right? Wouldn't you want at least one big hairy guy in *your* travel party? Plus, Jake Bixby has a growing sense about Marco. The hacker's offer to carry the injured Lexi on his back through Stoneship Woods seems like a pretty positive sign.

Jake slings Marco's huge camping backpack over his shoulder. It has a bedroll attached.

"Yeah, I've been sleeping in the woods for about a week," says Marco.

Lexi, arms clamped over his shoulders, asks, "Was it scary?"

"No," says Marco, nodding at the pack. "I lay out a pretty good detection grid."

"Excellent!" says Lucas, who leads the way with a

sleek-looking metallic flashlight. "I'd like to examine any gadgets you might have and then, like, log their functions and operative mechanisms in my personal notebooks."

Marco shakes his head. "You're a geek," he says.

"Yes, I am," says Lucas proudly.

"Then of course, so am I," says Marco, smiling ever so slightly. As if to demonstrate this point, he pulls his night-vision goggles down over his eyes.

They trudge forward. En route the Bixbys quiz Marco on his experience in the custody of the dark-suited agents. He recounts how the men drove him to a small, secluded airstrip. There they put him aboard a small black jet that took off and, he's pretty sure, flew in circles for several hours.

"It was *weird*, man," he concludes.

"How so?" asks Jake.

Marco halts suddenly and looks around.

"Did you hear that?" he asks.

Jake and Lucas freeze. They look around too.

After a few moments Jake says, "I don't hear anything."

"Me neither," says Lucas.

Everyone looks at Lexi, up on Marco's shoulders. She just shrugs.

"Okay," says Marco, walking again. "Anyway, to answer your question, they uncuffed me and started asking tough questions."

"Like what?"

"Like, what was I doing, trying to bring down the Internet? Stuff like that."

"Was there torture involved?" asks Lucas, looking a little queasy.

"No," says Marco gravely. "They spoke rudely, however. They even looked askance at me a few times."

Lexi laughs.

Marco says, "What?"

"You crack me up," she says.

"Good," says Marco. "Now stop digging your claws into my neck."

Jake grins a bit. "What did you tell them?"

"Everything."

"Good for you."

"Yeah, well, I'm not a very good liar." Now his tone darkens. "And anyway, I felt like a patsy, a fall guy. The whole Internet attack thing was a setup. So I told them all about Viper—a guy I've never met, by the way."

"Really?"

"Never seen him."

"How did he recruit you, then?"

"Secure chat room," says Marco with a hint of anger. "He hacked right into our network one day. Me and the guys, we were pretty impressed. We thought he was one of us, until things got to an advanced stage."

"Then he got abusive," says Jake.

Marco turns his goggle-eyes to Jake. "How did you know that?"

"We bugged your farmhouse," grins Jake.

Lexi slaps Marco on the shoulder. "Me again," she says.

"Anyway," says Marco, "the minute I spilled the beans on Viper, their little doggy ears perked up. It's like they didn't even care about our Internet project. All they wanted was Viper stories—how he contacted us, how he kept in touch, how he operated, and so on, and so on." He shakes his head. "Once I finished, they landed the jet, drove me back to Carrolton, and dropped me off in the Soccer Complex parking lot." He shrugs. "Then they drove away."

There is a significant pause. Then Jake finally asks the obvious question.

"So," he says, "who *were* those guys?"

Marco shrugs and says, "Got any guesses?"

"Government guys?"

"No!" calls Lucas from up front.

Marco frowns at him. "Why not?"

"If they were government guys," says Lucas, "they would have tortured you."

Marco lets out a loud laugh. The laugh's sonic wave splits and morphs into the sound of primeval tree squids, barking from above. This is due to the Doppler effect of the ambient frequency modulation, something I really don't understand, so please, can we just move on now?

Look, the point is this:

Stoneship Woods is a strange place, and no place to be after the sun goes down.

A few minutes later, Lucas halts.

Aha! This is the clearing just south of the warehouse perimeter fence. In the gathering darkness, things look different, of course. But the immense cottonwood is unmistakable, and as Lucas moves forward again, he spots the path he took through the foliage and pushes aside the low branches.

Soon his flashlight beam illuminates the jagged hole in the fence.

"Here we go!" he calls out.

Aren't you guys here yet? whines Cyril in both Bixbys' Spy Link earpieces.

"Yes, we are," says Jake. "South perimeter. Open the cargo door."

Shouldn't we follow established procedure? asks Cyril nervously. You know. Just in case it's not you?

"What?!"

Look, I see a light in the south surveillance feed, says Cyril. But how do I know it's you?

"Because I'm telling you we're here!" says Jake.

It could be a ruse.

"Cyril!"

You know, Jake, we set our protocol and procedures for a reason.

"Oh for dog's sake," says Jake as he pushes Marco's back-pack through the fence hole and sighs. He climbs through the hole and then turns to help Lucas crawl through. "Okay, okay," he says, "whatever." Then he says, "Lucas . . ."

"Got it," says Lucas.

The younger Bixby turns over his flashlight to reveal text entry buttons, a small messaging window, and the words Spy NightWriter etched on the handle. He punches a quick message into the keyboard and holds up the flashlight. Then he waves it briskly side to side. In glowing red letters, a scrolling message appears in the air:

OPEN UP, YOU PUSILLANIMOUS TOAD!

There's a pause. Then they hear Cyril say, That's not the protocol code.

"Open the cargo door, Cyril," says Jake quietly.

Okay, okay, says Cyril. You don't have to yell!

As Lexi and then Marco clamber carefully through the torn perimeter fence, the large cargo door slides open on the dark wall of the warehouse, creating a crack of light that slowly expands to a warm, glowing rectangle.

The thick-snouted quadraped, rising on its hind legs, mauls the sky as the surrounding meadow grass shudders in wild frenzy. Then the light blinds the camera. As the MPEG video file plays on, sullen darkness returns and the grass eddies and then calms.

With the console mouse, Cyril clicks the onscreen

Scan/Rewind button on the video playback interface, then freezes the frame where the creature's silhouette is most visible. Everyone stares in silence. Then Cyril points at the screen.

He says, "You know, people should keep better track of their pets."

Nearby, Lucas is visibly stunned. He frowns over at Lexi, who lies on the floor staring blankly at the screen. Her ankle, wrapped in a blue icepack from Marco's first aid kit, is elevated and resting on a chair.

Lucas points at the monitor.

Lexi just nods.

"What?" says Cyril, spinning his chair to face the younger kids.

"That creature's in the game!" says Lucas. "In M3! It's an überboss called the Slorg." He shakes his head in disbelief. "Lexi says it's vicious. Nobody at school has beaten it yet."

"What game?" asks Marco.

Lucas fills him in on The Massively Multiplayer Mystery and the odd, inexplicable appearance of Stoneship Woods and the steamy cave in the game's onscreen cybergeography.

"Okay, so this is getting weird," says Cyril.

Standing behind him, Marco nods grimly. He points at the beast on the big monitor.

He says, "I've seen that thing."

"When?"

"Several times."

"In these woods?" asks Jake, wide-eyed, standing next to Marco.

Marco gives him a look. "Yes," he says.

This brings a chill to the room.

"Where, exactly?" asks Jake.

"Mostly down in the cave."

Stunned, Cyril spins in the captain's chair. "You went *into* the cave?"

"Yes."

"By yourself?"

"Yes."

"Are you insane?"

Marco thinks about this.

Cyril starts to speak, then hesitates. He looks at the video screen and says, "That's not, like, an actual beast, is it?" He looks at Marco. "I mean, there's no such thing as an actual Slorg, right?"

Marco shrugs.

"Did it attack you?" asks Jake.

"No."

"Did it see you?"

"Yes," says Marco. "But it moves with a purpose." He leans closer to the screen, examining the creature. "It's active only at night, I think. I've never seen it in daylight."

Jake nods. "Well, whatever it is, maybe the black helicopter was looking for it at the cave."

"Maybe," says Marco.

"Or maybe they're looking for you again," says Lucas to Marco.

Marco nods slowly. "Maybe," he says.

Lucas points at Marco's goggles. "Nice optics, by the way," he says. "COMSPEC?"

Marco pulls off his headgear and hands it to Lucas. He says, "Generation Three, enhanced."

"Sweet!" Lucas examines the gear with deep reverence. "What's your scan rate? Twenty? Thirty?"

"Forty," says Marco.

Lucas whistles in admiration. "Wow! So what are your thoughts on that new phased-array thermal imaging technology?"

Cyril shouts, "Guys, could we get back to our primary topic? You know, regarding the huge honking fang-creature that apparently lurks nearby?"

Lucas hands back the goggles. "Okay, so why'd you explore the cave? Why are you hanging out in the woods?"

"Good questions," answers Marco.

After a pause, Lucas says, "Take your time."

"Let me think."

"About what?"

"About why I should trust you," says Marco. "You're just a bunch of little kids."

"Little kids?" says Cyril, pointing. "Ha! We took you *down*, jack."

Marco smiles slightly. He looks over at Jake, who has waited patiently through this exchange. After a long moment, Marco finally nods and sighs.

"Okay," says Marco. "So I did a little research."

"Hacking, you mean," says Jake.

"Whatever."

Jake grins. "Let me guess. Viper?"

"Yes."

"What'd you find?"

"Viper's tracks are almost impossible to follow," says Marco.

"Almost."

"Yeah, almost."

"So what led you to the cave?" asks Jake.

"Some interesting satellite photos."

This grabs Cyril's attention. "Military?" he asks nervously.

Marco shakes his head. "No, and I'll spare you the sordid details," he says. "Let's just say that I'm really good, and I managed to track down one of Viper's more obscure data trails. Somehow, the dude has access to real-time satellite imagery that maps out the topography of these woods." He gestures all around them. "And his primary focus of interest seems to be that cave opening."

"Wow," says Lucas.

"So," says Jake, "you went into the cave looking for Viper clues."

Marco nods once.

"Do you think he has some connection to *that* thing?" asks Jake, pointing at the monstrous silhouette on the main monitor again.

"That's one theory."

"Hmmm," says Lucas. "If Viper is connected to the cave and the Slorg, and both of those things are in M3 . . ." His voice trails off. Then his eyes grow big. "Do you think Viper has anything to do with M3?"

"The game *is* freaking out kids," says Jake.

"Exactly!" says Cyril, grabbing his hair. "It's making people act . . . *responsible*."

"It seems to be controlling behavior," agrees Jake.

Everybody looks at Jake for a second.

"*Exactly!*" shouts Cyril again. He tries to extricate his fingers from his hair, but fails.

"I wonder if we could investigate the game somehow," says Jake, with a glance over at Marco.

Marco nods. "You want me to hack the code."

"Well, Marco, that would be illegal."

"Consider it done."

Jake grins as Cyril seizes the mouse and scans forward on the Grendel video. This time he freezes the frame where the blinding red light from above first hits the creature.

"So, homeboys, do we conclude that this light"—Cyril points at the screen—"shines from the black helicopter we just saw?"

Jake nods. "Most likely."

Lucas stares at the screen again. He nods slowly too, but a hint of uncertainty lingers in his eyes. Jake notices this.

"Don't you agree?" asks Jake.

"Well, yeah," says Lucas, leaning closer to the screen. "But the light here is pretty *reddish*, and the actual helicopter light was more green like, wasn't it?" He frowns. "But I guess that's probably just a gamma correction thing, due to some compensation in the Minicam feed."

"Makes perfect sense to me," nods Cyril. "Although as usual, I have no idea what you're talking about."

Lucas glances over at Lexi. Ever since viewing the video, she has been very quiet. Her hands are wringing each other again.

Lucas crouches down by his pal.

"What is it, man?" he asks.

Lexi looks at him. Her pupils are dilated wide, so her dark eyes look pure black.

"Tell me, dude," says Lucas.

Lexi looks down at her hands. Then she holds them up. They tremble.

"Why do I keep doing this?" she asks forlornly.

"I think something's messing with your mind," says Lucas.

Now Jake crouches down next to Lucas. Lexi looks over at him.

She asks, "Why am I so scared?"

"Well," says Jake gently, "whatever that thing is"—he gestures at the monitor—"it's pretty dang scary."

"But why is it in the game?" asks Lexi.

Lucas nods and says, "And why is its cave in the game?"

"Actually," interrupts Marco, "it's not a cave per se."

"Really?" says Jake. "What is it?"

Marco squints over at Jake. He says, "An underground ventilation system."

"What does it ventilate?"

"I don't know."

Cyril's eyes widen at this. He says, "Is it easy to navigate?"

"No," says Marco. "It's a twisted mess. Kind of like, I don't know . . ."

"A maze?" asks Cyril hopefully.

"Yeah," says Marco. "You know, dead ends and stuff." He tucks his night-vision goggles into a side pouch on his huge backpack. "Like something you'd need a map to get through."

Cyril leaps up from his chair and punches the air. "Yesssss!" he hisses. He dances around a bit.

Marco is amused by this display. "What's up with the mophead?" he asks.

"Yeah, Cyril, what's up?" asks Jake.

Cyril drops back into the captain's chair and puts his fingers over the console keyboard. Then he starts typing and mouse-clicking like a madman.

"Lexi," he says, "can we get your avatar back alive in the game?"

"Of course!" cuts in Lucas impatiently. "When your guy dies in M3, he just transports back to your last save point in the game, right?"

Lexi nods.

"Excellent!" says Cyril. "Give me your password, Lexi."

Marco watches Cyril work. "What are you doing?" he asks.

Cyril, tapping away, says, "I'll bet a gazillion bucks that the real-world ventilation maze you found in the cave is recreated in the game too." He waits for an M3 log-in screen to load. "And if it is, we can solve it and map it. Then you can use our maze-map to navigate the actual ventilation pipes." He looks around. "I mean, guys, look at us. The total combined gaming experience present in this room is staggering."

Lexi pulls herself up and leans on Cyril's chair. The others crowd in behind him again. Suddenly, a cell phone rings.

"Oh my gosh!" cries Jake. It's his phone, and he pulls it out of a pocket.

Lucas looks aghast. "We didn't check in!" He looks at Cyril. "Did we? Did we check in?"

"No," says Cyril grimly, as if pronouncing a death sentence. "No, Lucas. You didn't check in."

Jake pushes the answer button on the phone. He takes a deep breath.

"Hi, Mom!" he says brightly.

Many painful minutes later, Jake finally manages to end the phone call.

"Yeah, love you too," he says for the tenth time. "Yeah, uh-huh, uh-huh. Uh-huh. Uh-huh. Uh-huh, uh-huh. We will. Yes. Okay. Love you too. *Bye!*"

He punches the End button and slumps to the floor. Finally, after some recovery time, he sits up and turns to the others.

"Mom says we gotta go home," he reports.

"Roger," says Lucas. "Let's scoot." He looks over at Cyril. "Sorry, man. We'll have to take a crack at the M3 cave maze later."

"Yeah," says Jake. He stands and claps a hand on Cyril's shoulder. "Like, tomorrow, right after school."

Cyril nods. "Cool," he says.

Jake notices Marco staring at the Stoneship command console—buttons, switches, monitors, readouts—and looking very thoughtful. Then he turns and surveys the other spectacular equipment and Spy Gear gadgets in the control room.

Finally Marco says, "You think it's just coincidence all

this stuff is here, in these woods, here in Carrolton? And Viper seems interested in this area too?"

Jake raises his eyebrows. He's been musing about the same thing for weeks, but he lets Marco play out his line of thought.

Marco points at the gadget shelf across the room.

"I mean, that stuff is sick," he says. "It's higher-tech than anything I've ever seen."

Cyril reaches behind his chair.

"Okay," he says. "Have a look at this, old man." Cyril holds up the Omega Link and hands it to Marco. "Check it out. Does this gibberish mean anything to you?"

The Omega Link! Wow. In all the excitement, we *completely* forgot about it. Thank goodness Cyril is here.

Jake and Lucas eagerly crowd in behind Marco to look at the strange collection of markings on the Omega Link display screen. Even Lexi limps over to take a peek.

Marco holds up the device. "What is this thing?" he asks. "Nobody knows."

Marco glances at Lucas and says, "Not even you, eh?"

Lucas shakes his head. "But messages just *appear* on it— clues, actually—so it's some sort of com-link." He gives Marco a look. "It helped us figure out what you were up to, as a matter of fact."

"Really?" says Marco. "Well, then." He looks at the

screen again. "Those look like Roman numerals, followed by, what—page numbers, maybe? Some kind of code, I guess." He looks at Cyril. "Did you guys look for a code book around here?"

"Of course we did," says Cyril. "We're professionals, Marco."

Marco nods. "Okay," he says. He looks at the odd numbers one more time. "I'm stumped."

"You think *those* are weird," says Cyril. "The last clue we got was just one character long—a dang *comma*, we think."

"A comma?"

Cyril nods. "Either that or a picture of six guys holding a squid, but shrunk *incredibly* small."

Marco looks over at Lucas and says, "What does a comma do?"

"In a sentence?" asks Lucas. "It's a . . . pause."

"Right."

"So it's telling us to pause? Pause what?"

Marco shrugs.

"Hey, really, we *gotta* get out of here," says Jake. He holds up his cell phone. "Unless you want to call my mom back."

"*No!*" shouts Cyril. "Please! I'd rather pour hydrogen peroxide on twenty paper cuts."

Lexi gingerly tries to walk a few steps. "I think I can walk," she says.

Marco looks down at her ankle.

"No way," he says. "That looks like a mutant pome-granate already."

With some Bixby help, Marco hefts Lexi up onto his back again.

Did we mention how creepy Stoneship Woods is? Like, at night and stuff?

Cyril is so stiff with fear that he walks like the Tin Man in desperate need of an oilcan. He looks over at Marco and mumbles through gritted teeth, "Tell us more about that wacky cave maze."

"Yes, distract us, will you?" asks Lucas.

Marco, with his night-vision goggles over his eyes, stops for a second.

"Did you hear that?" he asks.

"Hear what?"

Everybody stops. Nobody moves. For a few seconds the only sound is a light breeze whispering words of death in the branches above.

Then a small branch cracks.

Some twigs crunch.

Fallen leaves swish: *Swish!*

"Something's following us," says Marco calmly. He turns his goggled head side to side.

"Light!" calls Jake.

Lucas responds, aiming his flashlights beam into the trees along the path behind them. Nothing. Then he kills the light and pulls a Nightspyer mini-lens from a side pocket of his cargo pants and brings it to his eye. For a minute Marco and Lucas scan the surrounding foliage with their night-vision aids. Again, nothing.

"This way!" says Marco, moving quickly now. "We'll follow the old road out."

Marco takes the lead, crashing off the path into a tight thicket of birch trees. The hikers duck through white-bark trunks and leafless branches that rise like giant pale skeletons in the moonless sky. Behind them, the sounds of pursuit are unmistakable now—and getting louder.

"Hurry!" says Marco urgently.

Jake hears Marco's tone and feels a tsunami wave of fear wash over him. But he checks the urge to just run wildly through the trees. Instead, he drops slightly behind Lucas and Cyril, who trail Marco/Lexi.

If something is coming at them from behind, Jake plans to be the team's rear guard.

Kids, there's an old saying about courage that just happens to be true, so don't ever forget it.

Courage isn't the lack of fear. It's doing the right thing when you are scared to death.

Jake realizes that Marco is making a dead-reckoning beeline for the warehouse access road, an asphalt drive-way now cracked and overgrown with weeds. Jake understands this move. His impulse too is to escape the suffocating tangle of Stoneship trees, to push out into some open space where everybody can follow their deepest instinct and run like insane gazelles.

Behind, the pursuit grows closer. Jake can hear deep, guttural panting now.

Something's out there!

It's coming! It's coming!

Up ahead, Marco finally bursts from the thicket out onto the old road.

"Come on! *Run!*" he shouts.

The others crash through the last limbs and break into a terrified sprint down the road. Jake, running behind Lucas, looks wildly over his shoulder . . . just in time to see a dark figure explode from the trees and drop to all fours in the middle of the road. This gives Jake a surge of adrenaline. But then, almost immediately, he senses a new threat. He feels it in the pit of his stomach before he actually hears it—the fierce, rhythmic throbbing of powerful blades.

"Marco!" yells Jake. "The black helicopter!"

"Stay in the road!" shouts Marco, clomping along with a petrified Lexi clinging to his neck.

"But the spotlight—!"

"*Stay in the road!*"

Now the downward wash of air stirs the weeds and trees lining the access road. Jake risks another backward look as he runs. Whoa! The dark creature is gone! But now the menacing whine of chopper blades seems to come from all directions.

Where is it?

Behind? In front?

Above? Below?

Okay, maybe not below.

But Jake can get no bearing on the sound as its harsh intensity grows.

Cyril runs with surprising speed for a guy with rubberized legs and a hair-mop that frequently throws him off-balance. His lockjaw fear has kept him dead silent as he flails along behind Marco. But this deadly new incursion is just too much.

"Holy barking dogfish!" he shrieks.

Marco glances back. "Hang in there, kid!" he says. "We're almost out."

Up ahead, a neat row of tightly spaced trees blocks the entrance where the warehouse access road once connected to County Road 44. This, of course, is another mystery. These trees are obviously freshly planted, despite being fairly mature—indeed, some are almost twenty feet high. Clearly, planting them was a major operation. The manmade spacing is so tight that each runner must stop to wedge between tree trunks.

Jake hits this tree barricade last. As he squeezes through a gap, a maelstrom of dead leaves suddenly whirls around him. Branches shake violently. He feels the wild rush of air from above. Then, just as he finally rams through to the County Road, a blinding brightness bursts into his eyes from dead ahead.

Twin spears of white light—low, almost at ground level—seem to pierce him.

Jake sees his companions frozen in place, silhouetted in the cruel glare of the lights.

Trapped!

But then something very strange happens.

Although the blinding lights do not move, the harsh whine of chopper blades recedes. Somewhere up above, the airship is rising! Jake looks up but cannot see it. Then, suddenly, the sound whooshes away.

The rush of air just . . . stops.

Up ahead, the low drone of an automobile engine can be heard now, humming behind the high beams. Jake hears a car door open. As his eyes adjust, he can see the murky outline of a man emerge from the vehicle.

There is a pause that lasts a decade. Finally the outline speaks:

"Hi, kids!"

And then Mr. Latimer steps forward into the glare of his Toyota Avalon's headlights.

"Need a ride home?" he asks.

Cyril collapses into a pile of clammy body parts that will take hours to reassemble.

FUN WITH *BEOWULF*

The next morning, Jake and Cyril discuss the helicopter chase as they claw their way down the central hallway of Carlos Santana Middle School. "So you don't think Mr. Latimer chased away the craft?" yells Cyril above the mooing din.

"Highly doubt it," shouts Jake. He lifts his feet off the hall floor and lets the packed melee carry him a few yards. "It flew away right after the creature disappeared, right?"

"You think it's tracking the beast, eh?" yells Cyril. His head snaps back momentarily as his hair gets caught in a scrum of sixth graders. The momentum flips him upside down. He rides the crowd with his feet sticking straight up for several seconds.

"That's my theory!" shouts Jake. "Ah, here's our exit." He thrusts his feet back to the floor and grabs Cyril's ankles.

With well-timed lunges, the boys extract themselves from the howling mob and roll into their Language Arts classroom.

Here they split up. The assigned seating is alphabetical, so "Bixby" and "Wong" are on opposite sides of the room. But their Spy Link headsets let the boys keep in voice contact.

This is unnatural, whispers Cyril in Jake's earpiece.

Jake sits at his desk and glances around.

Indeed, it is unnatural. Most of the kids sit quietly, hands folded on their desks next to neat, annotated copies of *Beowulf*. The silence is oppressive. But then, this has been happening for weeks now—again, since M3 hit the market and became the rage.

Jake nods and says quietly, "It's too quiet."

"Ssshhhh!" says Megan Loudenbark, finger to her lips, across the aisle. She bares her teeth at Jake. Two fangs extrude.

"Whoa!" says Jake, leaning away from her. He glances over at Cyril, who looks pale.

"Sssssssssss!"

Jake turns to Tommie Smorch, who is hissing at him. Then Tommie carefully opens his copy of *Beowulf* and starts reading. After a few seconds he begins to hyperventilate and slams the book shut. He picks up a sharp pencil. Then he rips open the book and repeatedly stabs a page with the pencil.

Jake, watching this, mutters, "That's messed up, man."

The bell rings. Everybody freezes.

The silence is perfect.

Suddenly, Mrs. Scrotly bursts through the classroom door.

Mrs. Scrotly has been teaching *Beowulf* to eighth graders for twenty-five excruciating years. *Beowulf*, of course, is one of the grisliest, bloodiest, most gruesome tales in all of Western literature. Until this autumn, Mrs. Scrotly's *Beowulf* lesson plan usually consisted of reading a few lines out loud and then dragging nauseous kids to the Nurse Room.

Yet, as we mentioned in Chapter 1, odd things are going on in Carrolton. For some strange reason, children have been *begging* for the *Beowulf* unit. Courtney Retchkiss even founded an after-school *Beowulf* Club, with long chapter readings and banquets where everybody gnaws on huge shanks of undercooked meat.

So there's a new bounce in Mrs. Scrotly's walk this semester. Right now, for example, kids (and these are *eighth graders*, mind you) sit up straight and open their books the moment Mrs. Scrotly appears in the classroom doorway. Cyril and Jake, who slump deeply in their seats, give each other a look across the room. But they dutifully open their books too.

"Now, where were we when we left off?" begins Mrs. Scrotly.

"Section Eleven!" shout eager students simultaneously.

"Section Eleven! Section Eleven! Section Eleven!"

As Mrs. Scrotly notes this remarkable enthusiasm, a tear creeps into her eye. She heaves a heavy sigh of happiness.

"Yesss!" she whispers with a hint of ecstasy. "Yes, *precisely* that. Section Eleven."

"Yo, Scrotly!" calls Brill Joseph. "I'm perusing the table of contents, which is *fascinating*, by the way, and all I see is, like, a bunch of capital letters."

Mrs. Scrotly eyes him warily. But not even Brill's sneering disrespect can dampen her enthusiasm on this fine day.

"Mr. Joseph," says Mrs. Scrotly, "those are what educated people call 'Roman numerals.'"

"These are *numbers?*" asks Brill incredulously. "That's stupid!"

"No, it's not," says Mrs. Scrotly patiently. "Section Eleven would be the big *X* and the big *I*. See? Right next to each other!" She holds up her book to show him, smiling like a lobotomized mongoose.

At his desk, Jake Bixby stares down at this page. He squints hard at the Roman numeral: XI.

Then, suddenly, his eyes widen.

Excited, he looks across the room at Cyril, who frowns back with an expression that says, *'S up, dude?*

"Romans are stupid!" shouts Brill. He looks around the classroom, laughing *"Harl! Harl! Harl! Harl, harl!"* like a wolf with a tracheotomy. (Kids, please don't give your wolf a tracheotomy just to see what Brill sounds like.)

But nobody as much as glances at Brill, not even Wilson Wills, his bully sidekick, who sits across the room, right in front of Cyril. Wilson's eyes are glazed. Interestingly enough, Wilson spent an hour playing M3 at home before breakfast.

"That's what we call an 'inappropriate remark,' Mr. Joseph," says Mrs. Scrotly, who is pleased at the wonderful and frankly bizarre restraint shown by the rest of the class. "I'm sure Romans would find it most offensive. Now, who would like to start reading Section Eleven?"

Jake thrusts his arm into the air.

Cyril, stunned, stares at Jake with his jaw hanging open.

Most of the other kids raise their hands too. A few girls wave their arms wildly, sobbing and begging to be chosen. But Jake was first, and Mrs. Scrotly likes to be fair about these things.

"Mr. Bixby," she says.

Jake stands up, clears his throat, and gives Cyril a quick glance. Then he says, "Section Eleven, yes, that's X and I, lines *one* and *two*."

And he reads:

Then from the moorland, by misty crags,
With God's wrath laden, Grendel came.

Grendel, of course, is the fearsome monster that terrorizes everyone until the great hero Beowulf, in a poetic passage of delicate, stunning beauty, rips off one of its arms.

As Jake reads on, the huge creature enters the hall of warriors:

> **Straightway he seized a sleeping warrior**
> **for the first, and tore him fiercely asunder,**
> **the bone-frame bit, drank blood in streams,**
> **swallowed him piecemeal: swiftly thus**
> **the lifeless corpse was clear devoured,**
> **e'en feet and hands.**

Holy monkfish eggs! gasps Cyril in Jake's ear. **That's harsh.**

Jake glances around the room. Kids are transfixed with fear. He reads on. Later in Section XI, after Beowulf mortally wounds Grendel, Jake stops for a second, gives Cyril another significant look across the room, and says loudly, "Lines thirty-one to thirty-three."

"You really don't need to give us the line numbers, dear," says Mrs. Scrotly, chewing loudly on a wad of aluminum foil.

"Okay," says Jake. Then he reads:

> **To Beowulf now**
> **the glory was given, and Grendel, death-sick,**
> **thence sought his den in the dark moor:**

Jake looks over at Cyril and repeats slowly, "His den in the dark moor."

Cyril nods. Interesting, he murmurs in Jake's ear.

"That was lovely, Mr. Bixby," says Mrs. Scrotly. "You may sit."

The class bursts into applause.

"Thank you," says Jake, bowing. "Thank you. Thank you so much."

In his ear, Jake hears Cyril say, Time to call a lunch sit-rep, dude.[6]

The typical lunch hour at Carlos Santana Middle School features running, kicking, yelling, fighting, desperate fleeing, tactical retaliatory strikes, and sometimes even lunch. Today, the three boys of Team Spy Gear gather at the picnic table between the boccie goals and the curling sandpit, or whatever those things are. Lexi is nowhere to be seen.

Lucas opens his lunch sack and looks inside. Something reaches out and slaps him on the nose.

"Ouch!"

"Calamari again?" asks Cyril.

Lucas shuts the sack. "Got any spare food?" he asks Cyril.

Cyril checks his sack. "I've got a whole bag of Holios," he says.

6. For you kids who aren't in the Marines or army, "sit-rep" is short for "situational report," defined as an update to an existing situation as events unfold.

117

"What are those?"

"Small pockets of air surrounded by hydrogenated rice foam."

"Tasty!"

Jake eyes his sack warily. He holds his face away as he opens it.

"Whew!" he says. "Nothing got me."

He reaches inside and pulls out what appears to be an apple. Everyone looks at it.

"What is it?" asks Cyril, chewing on a Holio.

"It appears to be an apple," says Jake.

Cyril frowns. "Did your mom make that lunch?"

"Yes," says Jake. He holds up the so-called apple, examining it closely from various angles. Then he shakes it.

"You know, guys," he says, "it really appears to be an apple."

Cyril shakes his head in amazement. "I have never seen such normal food in a Bixby lunch sack before," he says.

Mrs. Bixby is infamous for her "gourmet" lunches. She once packed sandwiches made from a Moldavian cheese that cleared out the entire playground. Principal Krebsklaw had to call in a Hazmat team for collection and disposal.

Jake takes a bite of the crisp, juicy apple and says, "Okay, let's get down to business." He looks at Lucas. "So where's Lexi?"

Lucas shrugs. "Don't know."

"Son, it's your *job* to know," says Cyril.

"She's aware of the meeting," says Lucas. "I mean, I told her. In math."

"Call her via Spy Link."

Lucas shakes his head. "She decided not to wear the headset during school hours anymore."

"What?" shouts Cyril.

Lucas shrugs again. "She says it's too distracting. She needs to focus on stuff. Like, her studies and stuff."

Cyril is totally flabbergasted. "That's the most insane thing I've ever heard!"

"Maybe we should just go ahead without her," says Jake, glancing at his XP-6 Spy Watch. "We've only got fifteen more minutes of lunch break."

Lexi is missing the Team Spy Gear lunch meeting for a good reason.

Right now she lurks quietly in the Carlos Santana MS computer lab, watching kids play M3. And something strange is happening.

Technically, this gaming activity is not allowed. School policy allows connection to online sources from school computers for educational purposes only. But M3 seems to have such good cooperative aspects that even irritable Mrs. Burnskid looks the other way as kids crowd onto lab computers to join M3 clans, construct towns, barter and build economies, and establish healthy and secure cybercommunities such as Westhaven, home of Lexi's (or rather, Ralph the Mighty's) clan.

Indeed, M3 seems to offer plenty of good lessons for kids.

But today in the lab, tension is thick. Clan members are scared. Rumors abound of great beasts unleashed by enemy clans.

So Lexi, normally mesmerized by M3's onscreen action, watches the players themselves. Their talk turns to feuds, surprise attacks, enemy towns, raiding. War is openly discussed. Coalitions are forming, campaigns planned. Kids glance furtively at other kids: *What are they up to?*

Trust disintegrates. Fear rules.

Nearby, Taggert Biggles's avatar, one of Lexi's clansmen from Westhaven, has discovered the Slorg cave. Lexi eyes Taggert himself closely. When he prudently hits the Pause key at the first sight of the beast's red eyes, a red flashing reflects off his glasses and he suddenly stiffens.

At the next computer, Ashley Moan looks over and says, "There he goes again."

Lexi moves closer. Ashley turns sharply to her.

"They're out there!" she snarls. Then her head spins completely around.

"Whatever," says Lexi.

Lexi edges around Taggert's chair to see his face.

He sits blank-eyed, sweating.

Now Lexi feels fear crawl up the back of her own

throat like a Garbokki centipede. But she manages to swallow it back down, and if you've ever swallowed a Garbokki centipede you know just how hard that is because it really tickles quite a bit.

She forces herself to peek over at Taggert's monitor.

His warrior-avatar, Marge the Bonecrusher, is kneeling. As in most massively multiplayer games, a "paused" avatar is completely vulnerable to attack for sixty seconds until Taggert's account automatically logs off. An onscreen timer counts down the seconds: 45, 44, 43. But now something huge and dark emerges from the cave.

Lexi looks at Taggert again. "You won't make it to logoff," she says. "Trust me."

But Taggert cannot move.

"This is nuts," says Lexi. "Run!"

Taggert just sits there, hands trembling.

Lexi can't stand it anymore, so she reaches in and hits the spacebar to unfreeze Taggert's warrior. Then she directs the character away from the woods, running fast.

Taggert frowns and shakes his head. "Whoa!" he says, recovering a bit.

Lexi looks him in the eyes. He blinks a few times.

Then Ashley Moan says, "That happens *every* flipping time he pauses the game."

Lexi stares at Ashley. Her eyes suddenly widen with insight. "Pause," she says.

She stares down at the keyboard spacebar.

* * *

Cyril paces around the picnic table with furious intensity. Lucas watches, frowning.

"But what does it mean?" he asks.

Cyril says, "It's obvious, don't you think?"

"No."

"Grendel is *obviously* the Slorg," says Cyril. "And this 'den in the dark moor' has to be those ventilation shafts in the cave." He stops and nods. "Yes, that's where he lives, the den. But why does the Omega Link care about where the Slorg lives?"

Jake gives Cyril a skeptical look. He says, "Cyril, you don't really *believe* there's an actual Slorg?"

"Of course not!" says Cyril, glancing from brother to brother. "Do I look like some sort of hysterical paranoid lunatic?"

Jake and Lucas just gaze at Cyril.

"Okay, forget what I look like," says Cyril quickly. "The fact is, there is no such thing as a Slorg! As far as we know."

"Correct."

"But *clearly*," says Cyril, "it's probably, without a doubt, some guy, most likely, *dressed* as a Slorg, possibly." He raises his eyebrows a few times and adds, "Or so it would seem."

Jake pinches the spot between his eyes. He sighs and says, "Cyril, why would some guy dress as a Slorg and run around Carrolton, scaring the crap out of kids?"

"Because it's fun?"

Jake begins to speak, then stops. He thinks a moment. Then he has to nod. "Okay, so you actually have a point there."

"Or maybe it's some kind of publicity stunt," says Cyril.

"What do you mean?"

Cyril's smoking hot now. "Think about it! M3's publisher hires some guy to wear a Slorg suit. They tell him to lurk in neighborhoods with high-speed broadband connectivity and six-figure household incomes. His job: scare kids." Cyril nods, satisfied.

"What?" says Jake. He looks skeptically over at Lucas.

Lucas says, "I'd *love* to have that job."

"See?" says Cyril. "I'm not totally crackpot."

"Not totally," agrees Jake. He looks around. "So has anybody seen Lexi yet?"

"Maybe she went home for lunch today," says Cyril.

"Maybe."

Jake scans the school grounds. Dozens of kids line the east fence, pulling weeds. Others groom the volleyball pit with small combs. Then he notices Brill and Wilson huddled in a suspicious manner.

"Hmmm," he says. "What sort of foul scheme are those two bums concocting?"

Lucas suddenly brightens.

"Wanna find out?" he says slyly.

Jake grins. "What's up your sleeve, bro?"

Lucas opens the gadget backpack at his feet and pulls out a Spy Supersonic Ear, a directional sound dish with headphones attached. He slides on the headphones, activates the dish unit, and points it toward Brill and Wilson across the grounds.

In his ear, Lucas picks up their conversation. It quickly becomes clear that they're discussing plans for Halloween night, this coming Thursday:

Okay, dude, but you [censored] carry the [censored] cats this time, dude.

Hey, dude, let's nail both Bixbys instead! I hate those [censored].

Dude, where the [censored] should we spring the trap?

Dude, down by Platte Park. Those [censored] have to pass there if they work Ridgeview for all the primo Halloween candy. You still got those [censored] fireworks?

[Censored] yes! What, you think I'd [censored] throw them out?

Dude, we'll lure the [censored] Bixbys over to the tunnel slide, then throw down some bottle rocket madness.

Smackdown!

Dude, like, this ought to [censored] their [censored].

[Censored]! [Censored]!

[Censored] [censored], you [censored] [censored].

[Censored] too!

Harl harl harl harl harl!

Lucas pulls off the headphones.

"Those guys are idiots," he says.

"They're pretty good examples of what happens if you touch radioactive materials," says Cyril.

"What did they say?" asks Jake, smiling.

"Evil Halloween plans," says Lucas. "I'll give you the 411 later."

"Cool."

"I'm sorry," says Cyril, watching Brill grab a small boy and hold him upside down while Wilson steals the boy's spleen, "but anybody who doesn't believe in monsters and beasts is just in denial."

Jake nods. Then he says, "So anyway, Lucas, that's our take on the Omega Link message. Somehow *Beowulf* seems to be the code book. And I think it's no coincidence that the Slorg video at HQ was labeled 'Grendel.' Wouldn't you agree?"

"Yes, and keep in mind," adds Cyril, "that video was probably shot months ago, before Stoneship was abandoned. So that thing, whatever it is, has been roaming the woods for a long time."

"Maybe living in the cave," says Jake.

"Can I see the Omega numbers again?" asks Lucas.

"Sure." Jake digs in his bookpack. "I wrote them down uh—somewhere." He keeps digging. "Yeah, well, I know they're in here, you know, actually, somewhere."

Cyril opens his own pack.

"No worry," he says. "I took the liberty of bringing *this* bad boy." He pulls out the Omega Link itself. When he glances at its display screen, he frowns and then looks closer.

"Huh," he says. "Say Jake, didn't both of those messages start with Roman numeral eleven?"

"Affirmative," says Jake.

"Hmmm," says Cyril. "Check this out."

He hands Jake the Omega Link. There, etched on the screen, is the following:

$$XXII, \quad 38-45$$

Jake stares for a second, getting excited.

"These are new numbers!" he says. "Cyril!"

"Got it already," says Cyril, slapping his copy of *Beowulf* down on the picnic table. "What's the reference again?"

"Section Twenty-two, lines thirty-eight to forty-five."

Jake sets the device on the table; Lucas whips out a notebook and jots down the message exactly as it appears onscreen. Then the Bixbys watch as Cyril flips *Beowulf* pages to Section XXII. He moves his finger down the poem's verses, counting lines.

"Okay," he says. "It starts here."

"You read it," says Jake.

And Cyril reads the following lines:

Many sea-beasts
tried with fierce tusks to tear Beowulf's mail,
and swarmed on the stranger. But soon he found
himself in some underwater hall, he knew not which,
where water never could work him harm,
nor through the roof ever could reach him
fangs of the flood. Firelight he saw,
beams of a blaze that brightly shone.

"Sea-beasts with tusks?" says Cyril. He turns abruptly to Jake. "I have a question."

Jake, frowning as he leans over to reread the passage, says, "Yeah?"

"What is *wrong* with just, like, telling people what you want to tell them?" he asks. He grabs the Omega Link and glares at the screen. "Dude!" he yells at it. *"Talk straight to us!"*

As if in response, the Omega Link beeps.

The boys all stare at it. It beeps again.

Then the screen goes blank.

"Oh, *great*, Cyril," says Lucas irritably. "You hurt its feelings!"

Cyril goes pale. He is about to apologize when the Omega Link beeps a third time. And the following message appears:

X X X V I , 6 8 – 7 1

"Aha!" says Jake. "Cyril?"

Cyril flips quickly to the new section cited onscreen, turning *Beowulf* pages so fast he practically rips them out of the book. At Section XXXVI, he counts down to line 68 and reads aloud:

At the words the serpent came once again,
murderous monster mad with rage,
with fire-billows flaming, its foes to seek:
the hated men.

He reads it again slowly. This time he glances up at Jake as he repeats the words "serpent" and then "murderous monster."

"Who do you suppose *that* is?" he asks, his voice cracking.

"Serpent," says Jake darkly. "Take a guess."

Suddenly there's a crackle of static in the boys' Spy Link headsets. A voice says:

Breaker, breaker, Lima Bravo, do you read me?

Lucas brightens. "Ah, *there* you are, he says, putting his finger to the earpiece. "Where you been, dude?"

Computer lab, answers Lexi.

"Yeah? What up?"

I know what the comma means.

Lucas raises his eyebrows and looks over at Jake. He says, "Really?"

Lexi says, **And I know how to beat the Slorg.**

INTO THE DEN

Ralph the Mighty runs through the woods, feeling the wet heat of beast-breath on the back of his neck. Up ahead, a massive cottonwood tree looms above the other treetops. Its leaves flutter with green digital precision.

"There it is!" cries Lucas.

"The old cottonwood!" exclaims Cyril.

"Go, go, go!" shouts Jake. "The Slorg's gaining on you!"

Lexi, sitting at the Stoneship HQ console keyboard, guides Ralph into a familiar-looking clearing. Nearby, the three boys watch tensely. As the long-legged Ranger glides past the great cottonwood, he suddenly and deftly slides behind it. A hideous *chomp!* of powerful jaws is followed by the sound of splintering wood.

"Nice move!" says Cyril. "He bit the tree!"

Lucas nods at Lexi. "You just bought five seconds, dude. Phase One complete."

Onscreen, Ralph is off and running again. This time he follows a narrow, overgrown forest path. The beast is hot on his heels again, closing the distance. Ralph's stride is indeed mighty, however, so he manages to keep a step ahead of the Slorg.

Lucas consults his notebook. He says, "Okay man, bear left a bit. Stay sharp for Phase Two, guys! We're looking for a red monolith in another clearing, a smaller one."

Jake and Cyril both lean toward the monitor, watching intently. Onscreen, Ralph bursts into a small clearing where a huge chunk of red sandstone rises like a monument.

"There!" points Cyril. "There it is!"

Jake shouts, "Hit it, girl!"

Lexi steers Ralph directly at the huge red monolith. Again the snarling, drooling sound of a bloodthirsty pursuer rattles the console speakers. Onscreen, Ralph hits the rock running full speed—and then passes right through it!

Lexi quietly says, "*Yes!*"

"Okay, excellent, that's the first clipping error," says Lucas quickly, reading his notebook. "Now look for the yellow leafy patch. Everyone! Come on, people! Eyes peeled!"

"There it is!" shrieks Cyril, pointing. "Dead ahead!"

"I see it," says Lexi calmly.

* * *

Parents, I believe it's time for another brief computer gaming tutorial.

Put down your cell phones and listen up, please.

A "clipping error" is a type of programming bug in a videogame. When something that's supposed to be solid matter in the game world—say, an avatar like Ralph the Mighty, for instance—can pass like an incorporeal ghost right through something *else* that's supposed to be solid matter—like, say, a massive red boulder—you have one kind of clipping error.

But there are other types of clipping errors too.

Sometimes a clipping error becomes a kind of quicksand in a game. Characters can walk into objects or areas but can't walk out.

They get stuck.

Earlier this afternoon, after asking around in the school computer lab, Lexi learned that nobody—not even Carrolton's best M3 warriors and mages—could defeat the Slorg boss-beast in battle. However, Mookie Pickens, the biggest videogame geek in the school, told Lexi he'd found a "quicksand bug"—a clipping error that freezes movement.

"But it's almost impossible to lure the Slorg into the bug without getting, like, eviscerated," said Mookie. "You have to be *really* fast and *really* good to make it before the Slorg eats you, dude."

So Lexi arranged a meeting with Mookie after

school, where Lucas took notes on the exact route to this lucky glitch.

Lexi guides Ralph the Mighty directly toward the pile of yellow leaves . . . and then slows down slightly.

Behind, the Slorg's snarl is deafening. Clearly it has passed through the monolith too. The screen tint reddens as the beast wounds Ralph with a couple of talon-swipes from behind.

"Now!" screams Cyril. His legs give out and he falls to his knees, howling: *"By the beard of Zeus, jump! Jump! Jump!"*

Ralph, loping easily now, plants a foot just before the leafy patch. A spray of beast-bile and mucus hits the screen as the Slorg strikes. But at that precise moment Lexi hits the keyboard Jump key with a quick double-tap. Onscreen, Ralph leaps lightly over the yellow leaf pile. When he lands on the far side, he stops.

Behind him, the gruesome gut-wail of the Slorg is ear-splitting. But the sound comes no closer. Lexi slowly turns Ralph 180 degrees.

Onscreen, we see what Ralph sees. The first-person view swivels to reveal the murderous, red-eyed Slorg flailing just ten feet away.

But the beast is running in place, half-sunken in the yellow leaf patch.

Stuck!

"And *there's* the second clipping error," says Lucas,

exhaling with gusto. He beams large at the screen. "Phase Two complete."

Jake grins at Lexi. "Mad, mad skills," he says.

Cyril, still on his knees, turns to Lexi too.

"I bow before the Master Dude," he says, lowering his hands to the ground.

Lucas whacks Lexi on the back. He says, "You rock the mob."

The Master Dude leans back in her chair. Yes, right now, Lexi Lopez is about as satisfied as she's ever been in her entire life.

"Okay, folks," says Lucas, clapping his hands to get everyone's attention. "Let's go to Phase Three."

Now that the M3 Slorg is immobilized, Phase Three is to map out the beast's underground den.

Again, Cyril's theory is that the Slorg's tunnel-maze in the game recreates the real-world underground air duct system that befuddled Marco. If you can map the game maze, you can use that map to navigate the ventilation maze.

A stretch? Perhaps.

But we've heard nuttier theories. For example, some people actually use the mathematics of differential geometry and tensors to describe gravity, making it not a force but rather a consequence of the curvature of space-time, and then postulate that the presence of mass and energy actually "curves" space-time, and this curvature affects the path of free particles, even light!

Ha! Isn't that the most preposterous thing you've ever heard?

In any case, the *Beowulf* "code book" clues (courtesy of the Omega Link) all point to the Slorg den. And as Marco reported, Viper himself seems involved, based on his interest in the actual underground cave system—interested enough to maintain expensive satellite surveillance of the cave mouth.

And strangest of all, the cave and woods have been digitally recreated online in a wildly popular game.

Geez, what more evidence do you need?

"Something's down there," says Jake. "Something important, I think."

Of course, before now, the problem with mapping the Slorg cave in M3 has been the ferocious presence of the seemingly invincible Slorg, who guards his cave entrance jealously.

But now Ralph the Mighty stands unmolested at the cave mouth.

"Ready to spelunk, sir," says Lexi.

"Let's go map-mode," says Lucas excitedly.

"Roger that," says Cyril.

He slings open his laptop and clicks open a program called GameGeek 3-D Mapmaker. This nifty software lets you create three-dimensional maps as you move through the cyberspace of a game world. As Lexi guides Ralph down the dank underground passages of the cave maze leading to the Slorg den, Cyril taps away, building his "map space" based on Ralph's every movement.

The maze is tricky, but with Cyril's mapping prowess and so many veteran videogamers providing input, Ralph makes swift progress.

One hour into the maze solution process, Jake notices something moving on one of the console's surveillance feeds. He turns and watches with concern for a second, but then relaxes.

"Look, Marco approaching the south door," he says, pointing at the side monitor.

Cyril reaches over and hits a console button to open the cargo door. Seconds later, Marco pushes his bedroll through the control room floor hatch and then pops his head up.

"Wow," says Cyril. "You look terrible."

"Shut up." Marco rubs his forehead. "I really hate nosy brats."

Marco pulls himself through the hatch and sees the M3 game on the main monitor. "Yes, that's the *best* use of this sophisticated equipment. When you're done, be sure to play some Solitaire, too."

Lucas quickly reiterates their theory that the game maze mirrors the ventilation system.

"Right," says Marco. "Next you'll be telling me that *E* equals *MC* squared."

Cyril points to the monitor. "Check it out," he says. "*You've* been down there. Does it look familiar?"

Marco eyes the screen closely. "No, the air tunnels don't look anything like that," he says, nodding at the onscreen cave passages. "No stalagmites. No mossy rock protrusions."

"But does the *route* look familiar?" asks Jake.

"Hard to say," says Marco. "I was lost and babbling most of the time." He watches Ralph the Mighty suddenly spin and hack at some small tentacle-waving attackers. "What are those?"

Cyril says, "Squidlets."

Marco nods. "Didn't see any of those."

"Of *course* not," says Cyril. "In the game here, see, it's an evil monster's lair, and those are his fictional minions. Out there in real life, the cave's probably like, you know, it's, it's like quite a bit *different*, I would imagine, and mostly it's minus any squidlets or minions of any sort."

"No squidlets?"

"No, I don't believe so."

"That's too bad."

"Well," says Cyril. "I'm not really sure." He rubs his hair thoughtfully. "Maybe there's a few."

Marco just stares at Cyril. Then he checks his watch.

"Children," he says. "Remember: It gets dark early now." He looks at Jake. "Don't get in trouble with your mommy again, Bixby."

"We weren't in trouble," says Lucas defensively.

Marco just smiles.

"Don't worry, old man," says Jake to Marco with a sly grin. "The last thing *any* of us wants is to walk through these woods again at night."

Thirty minutes later, Phase Three is complete. Lexi says, "That's it, guys. Hitting Pause." Everybody averts their eyes from red onscreen flashes as she pushes the keyboard spacebar.

"The Omega Link really outdid itself with that clue," says Lucas. "A comma. *Pause.* Ha! Very clever."

"So what are those red flashes?" asks Jake. "How do they work?"

"Some kind of subliminal messaging, maybe," says Lucas. "Behavior modification. Possibly hypnosis." He shakes his head. "If so, this is some very sophisticated psy-ops."

Nearby, Cyril stares at his laptop screen and nods, satisfied. "Okay, guys, unless we're missing some super-secret passages," he says, "we've mapped just about every inch of this maze." He pushes a key to save the final 3-D maze map. "The big secret seems to be the Slorg's Treasure

Room, back here." He scrolls through the map to the location. "Of course, who knows what sort of room it might be in the *real* cave?"

Jake eyes the Slorg's piles of treasure onscreen. He says, "My guess is the real cave holds something far more interesting than Moldasso rubies and the Garbedian Power Orb."

Loud snoring suddenly draws their attention. It sounds like somebody letting the air out of a really huge party balloon.

Over in the corner, Marco is conked out with his head on his bedroll.

"Yikes," says Lucas, covering his ears. "He's out like a light."

"Dang, we need to scoot," says Jake with a nervous glance at his watch. "It'll be dark in half an hour."

"I'll wake him," says Cyril. "Anyone got a taser?"

"Let him sleep," says Lexi.

The boys all look at her.

Cyril says, "We can't leave him in here with all our stuff!"

"Why not?" asks Lexi.

"Because it's our stuff!"

Lexi looks confused. "It is?"

Jake smiles. He says, "She's got a point. Why make him sleep in the woods? It's not safe."

"But our stuff!" says Cyril. He puts his hand on the command console. "What if he, like, messes it up?"

Lucas is nodding now. "Cyril," he says, "Viper hired Marco to *bring down the Internet*." He glances over at the grubby, unconscious hacker. "My guess is he's one of the ten or twenty best computer nerds in the Western world." He looks back at Cyril. "I don't think he's gonna mess up your stuff."

Marco sucks in a lungful of air and rattles it out through thick, vibrating sheets of phlegm.

"That's *intense*," says Cyril, ducking.

"Let's go," says Jake. "Let the guy sleep." He looks over at Lexi, who jots something on a sheet of notebook paper. "What's that, man?"

"A note for Marco," she says, writing.

Jake nods. "Cool," he says. "Tell him that Phase Four begins here tomorrow at two forty-five, *immediately* after school. We need to get in and out of those tunnels before it gets dark."

Lexi finishes and folds the note. Then she looks at Jake. "What about the Slorg?"

"There's no such thing," says Jake reassuringly.

"Really?" says Cyril. "Then what's that *entity* in the Grendel video?"

"I don't know," says Jake. "But it's not a Slorg, Cyril."

"How do you know that?" says Cyril, his voice rising.

Jake grabs his buddy's shoulders and looks him right in the eye. He says firmly, "Because there's *no such thing* as a Slorg."

(13)

A NEGATIVE INCLINATION

The next day, Tuesday, October twenty-ninth, school seems to last *hours* for Team Spy Gear. Indeed, the day seems to go on *all day*.

The only thing that makes the waiting even remotely tolerable is the increasingly weird and perversely entertaining behavior of fellow Santana students. Oh, and also there's the moment when Lexi figures out the final Omega Link clue. That's kind of interesting too.

But we'll get to that in a minute.

First there's the morning arrival. It's raining, so Mrs. Bixby rolls out the family SUV and ferries her boys from 44444 Agincourt Drive to school. As Jake and Lucas slide down the pole from the passenger compartment and exit via the security hatch, Mrs. Bixby calls down, "Have a good day, boys!"

"We will," say the Bixby boys in unison.

"I love you! Have a good day!"

"Love you too," say the Bixby boys.

"I packed something special for lunch today!"

Jake and Luke exchange a look. "That would explain the odor," says Jake quietly.

"Thanks, Mom!" say the Bixby boys in unison.

"Love you!"

"Love you too, Mom!" say the Bixby boys in unison.

Behind them, traffic in the school drop-off circle backs up for miles.

"If it's still raining at three, Dad will leave work early and be waiting for you right here!" calls Mrs. Bixby from the cockpit.

"All righty, then!" say the Bixby boys in unison.

"Got your backpacks?"

"Yes."

"Okay, then!"

"Okay. Bye."

"Love you."

"Love you too. Bye."

"Bye-bye!"

Behind them, horns honk. People start throwing tomatoes and beets.

"Let's go," whispers Jake to Lucas.

The boys hurry into the school. They dive into the morning hall rush and start mooing.

* * *

Now things get really interesting.

Carlos Santana Middle School students are acting weird today, but in a new way. Many wear armbands signifying their M3 clan memberships. Clannish behavior is evident in other ways, too. Kids move around school in small circular packs, with guard units facing the rear and walking backward in a crouch. Halls are full of tension and accusations. Teachers look befuddled. It seems all of the good social aspects of M3 gameplay have evaporated, almost overnight.

When Team Spy Gear gathers at noon near the school's horseshoes velodrome, Lucas drops his backpack on the picnic table and says, "Whew! Everyone in this school has gone bonkers."

"No kidding," says Jake. "What's going on?"

Lucas pulls out his lunch sack. He says, "The M3 psy-ops must be kicking into a whole new level. Like, making kids *paranoid* now."

"Are you planning to open that sack?" asks Cyril warily.

"No."

"Good." Cyril gnaws on a carrot. "I really don't feel like fending off squidlet tusks."

Next to Lucas, Lexi takes a sip of Organic Torpedo Juice and watches a tetherball incident unfold on the playground. Then suddenly she frowns.

Lucas notices. "Bad juice?" he asks.

Lexi looks over at Cyril. "Tusks."

"What?" asks Cyril.

"In the game maze," says Lexi. "The squidlets. They had tusks."

Cyril nods. "Vicious little tusks, my friend. So what's your point?"

Then Jake's eyes widen. He turns to Lexi. He says, "'Sea-beasts with fierce tusks.'"

Lexi nods.

Without another word, Jake digs into his backpack and pulls out his *Beowulf* text. He opens to section XXII and reads aloud:

Many sea-beasts tried with fierce tusks to tear Beowulf's mail, and swarmed on the stranger.

He looks up at Lucas. "Sea-beasts! Could those be the squidlets in the game?"

"Possibly," says Lucas. "Or could be just coincidence. Read on."

Jake reads the next sentence of the verse:

But soon he found himself in some underwater hall, he knew not which, where water never could work him harm, nor through the roof ever could reach him fangs of the flood.

"What the blue donkey does *that* mean?" asks Lucas, scratching his head.

"Stumped here," says Jake.

"Same," says Cyril. "Although I'm getting tired of all these tusks and fangs and stuff."

Jake reads the last underlined sentence of the verse:

Firelight he saw, beams of a blaze that brightly shone.

Now Lexi frowns again. She says, "Firelight?"

"Right," says Jake.

Lexi says, "Huh."

"Does that word mean something to you?"

Lexi reaches into her backpack. As she digs around, the three boys exchange puzzled looks. Finally she yanks out a sheet of paper. "I printed this off the Internet," she says. She hands the paper to Lucas.

"It's a review of M3 from GameGeekoids.com," says Lucas, looking at it. "Plus game tips and an interview with the designers."

"Look here," says Lexi, pointing at the article.

Lucas reads for a second. "Huh," he says. He holds out the paper to Jake. "Check the name of the design group that created The Massively Multiplayer Mystery."

Jake reads: "Firelight Studios."

Now Jake picks up his copy of *Beowulf* and reads the last line again:

Firelight he saw, beams of a blaze that brightly shone.

He stares at Lexi, then at Lucas, and finally at Cyril. "Coincidence?" he asks.

"Right," says Cyril. "Just like the Slorg and the cave just *happen* to be in the game."

Jake looks back down at the article. "Good point," he says. "Clearly there's some connection between the Omega clues, the cave, the creature . . . and the dang game."

"Read this part of the interview," says Lexi, pointing at the page.

Jake reads out loud:

Q: Why is the location of your game design studio such a well-guarded secret? You guys aren't involved with organized crime, are you?

S: Yes, we have serious underworld connections. (laughs) Actually, we have some proprietary equipment that nobody should see.

Q: Got it.

S: But anybody with a negative inclination can find us.

Q: Care to offer any clues?

S: I just did. (laughs again) For superior M3 gamers, the route to our snake pit will be obvious.

"Underworld?" says Lucas. "Wow! Like, *underground* maybe?"

Cyril clears his throat. "And here, folks, is where it

pays to be Captain Math Geek," he says. "In my world, you see, a 'negative inclination' is a downward slope."

Jake beams at his buddy. "I think we're on to something," he says, nodding.

"Like what?" asks Cyril.

"Like maybe the location of Firelight Studios!" shouts Lucas. He starts bouncing up and down and rubbing his hands together in excitement. "It sounds perfectly plausible, doesn't it?" He looks over at Cyril. "An underground maze of ventilation tunnels leads to the hidden location of the leading game design studio in the world? And the maze route is right there in the studio's game? It makes perfect sense!"

"Sure," says Cyril, nodding his hair. "Any idiot could see that."

"Okay, it does sound far-fetched," says Jake, as he scans the article. "By the way, it says here that the lead designer chose to remain anonymous, so he used a nickname." He reads further. "The *S* in the interview stands for Snake."

Now Cyril frowns. "Snake?"

"Snake, yes."

"As in . . . *serpent*?"

Jake nods yes. "An example might be, say, a viper."

Team members exchange grim looks here. The Bixbys glance at the author, who raises his eyebrows to suggest they're on the right track, then cues Cyril to open *Beowulf* again.

146

Slowly Cyril rereads the section XXXVI passage:

**At the words the serpent came once again,
murderous monster mad with rage,
with fire-billows flaming, its foes to seek:
the hated men.**

There is a pause as these words sink in.

"Well," says Lucas finally. "*That* doesn't sound so good."

"No," says Jake, still looking at the passage. "No, it doesn't." He looks at Lucas. "It doesn't sound good."

Angry chants, clan versus clan, drift back and forth across the playground.

"Maybe we should re-think this deployment," says Cyril three hours later as he thrashes through the tangled, clutching limbs of Stoneship Woods. "Really, guys, I just really don't like the sound of this snake thing, not at all."

Now Team Spy Gear pushes out of the trees onto the asphalt access road and approaches the main entrance of the Stoneship Toys warehouse yard. The ten-foot-high chain-link entrance gate is topped with a nasty spiral of barbed wire, just like the rest of the perimeter fence that surrounds the yard.

"Don't tell me you're afraid of murderous monsters with fire-billows flaming?" says Jake.

Jake unzips a side pocket on his cargo pants and pulls out a small device that resembles a superdeluxe garage door opener. He pushes one of its buttons. The front gate slowly rolls open.

"Look, I admit that physical courage is not my strong suit," says Cyril. "But I hate snakes, Jake. I fear them insanely, in the most irrational manner possible. Almost as much as Lucas fears insects."

Lucas laughs. "Dude, *you'll* be mission control, as per usual," he says. "*I'll* be exploring the underworld."

Cyril claps Lucas on the shoulder. "Exactly," he says. "Which is an *excellent* plan, by the way." Cyril turns to Jake. "But my point is this. The Omega Link has been right about everything so far, hasn't it?"

"Pretty much," agrees Jake.

The four spies enter the fenced compound and veer left, heading around the south side of the warehouse building. Willowy weeds bend in a sudden cold breeze that blows across the overgrown yard.

Cyril shivers and says, "Well, frankly, that last *Beowulf* passage about the serpent sounds like more than just *guidance* to me." He gives Jake a serious look. "It sounds like a warning."

Jake nods. He hears Cyril's tone clearly. "So you think we shouldn't go down into the tunnels," says Jake.

Cyril says, "Right."

"You think Viper's down there?"

"Maybe."

"He's the murderous serpent?"

Cyril looks uncomfortable. "Maybe."

As Jake considers this, Lucas says, "Hey, the south door is open."

Sure enough, the south cargo door is wide open. The four approach and peer inside.

"Yo, Marco!" calls Lucas.

"Marco! Hey, Marco!"

No answer.

Without hesitation, Lexi runs to the recessed wall ladder and climbs. Her ankle is still tender, but a tight tape wrap (courtesy of her gymnastics coach) lets her move much like the old Lexi, only newer. Jake and the others follow. As Jake pulls himself up into the control room, he sees Lexi at the command console, alone.

She looks over at Jake and says, "He's gone."

"Did he steal any stuff?" yells Cyril, still climbing the ladder.

For the next minute or so, the team scours the control room, taking a quick inventory. Nothing seems to be missing. On the contrary, there's actually a new device on the command console: a small, handheld gadget with a Firewire data cable attached. Next to it is a shiny DVD-ROM disk, atop the note Lexi wrote to Marco yesterday.

"Looks like Marco read your note," says Jake to Lexi.

"And gee, he left us something," says Cyril. "But what is it?"

Everybody looks at Lucas.

Lucas picks up the gadget. He flicks a button. A small display screen lights up.

"Aha," he says. "It's a GPS receiver."

"A what?" asks Cyril.

Lucas hefts the gadget. "GPS stands for Global Positioning System," he says, sounding like a university professor, only really small, especially the feet. "It's a constellation of twenty-four satellites in geostationary orbits that continuously signal their positions. GPS devices like this unit can receive those satellite signals and then use them to compute your exact location on Earth." He grins. "So you can navigate anywhere and never be lost, even in the wildest jungles of Borneo."

Cyril nods. "I've been lost in Borneo, man," he says grimly.

"What's with the cable?" asks Jake.

Lucas picks up the cable's loose end. "Looks like you can plug the GPS unit into any computer that has a Firewire port," he says.

Cyril slings his backpack onto the command console and slips out his laptop.

"Like, say, this baby?" he says.

"Right," says Lucas. He picks up the shiny disk and reads the label. "This is GeoMapper 3.0, the latest version of GeoGrid's satellite imagery mapping software."

Lexi picks up the note. She turns it over.

"Hey, Marco wrote back," she says.

At this very moment Mr. Latimer casually trails a black BMW in his Avalon. He follows at a good distance, because he's pretty sure where it's headed: Stoneship Woods. And sure enough, that's where it stops.

Mr. Latimer parks two blocks away and watches.

After a very short time—maybe just a minute or two— two more black cars, long and identical, pull up behind the BMW. Nobody exits any of the cars.

After another couple of minutes, one of the long black cars pulls away from the curb, makes a U-turn, and parks again, this time facing the opposite direction.

Marco's note provides step-by-step directions for plugging the GPS unit into the Firewire port on Cyril's laptop and then installing GeoMapper 3.0. And Marco has included one more technical tip. It turns out that GeoMapper 3.0 can actually import files from GameGeek 3-D Mapmaker, Cyril's game-mapping program.

The note ends with a quick sign-off:

FOUND ANOTHER VIPER
TRAIL, MARCO OUT

"Must've left in a hurry," says Lucas.

Jake rereads the note. "He doesn't say anything about meeting up, or where to reach him," he says with a hint of disappointment.

Lexi, standing next to Jake, says, "I don't get it."

Jake looks down at her. "I don't either," he says.

"He's on our side, right?"

"I think so."

"Wow!" says Cyril, tapping away on his laptop. "See? I can create a transparent overlay of the M3 underground maze-map, the one we plotted yesterday, to real-world scale. Then I can import that overlay into GeoMapper and drop it directly on top of the actual satellite image of Stoneship Woods."

The others peer over his shoulder as he clicks madly on his laptop screen.

"Does that mean we can see where the Slorg tunnels might lead to in the real world?" asks Jake.

"Yes, exactly!" says Cyril. "Now, if I can find the actual ventilation cave entrance"—he scrolls the onscreen satellite image of Stoneship Woods, looking for the cave—"I can match up the coordinates. Then we can see where that 'Slorg Treasure Room' is actually located in the real world."

"This is sick," says Lucas in admiration.

Cyril clicks some more. "My guess is the tunnels end up in the basement of some building. If so, we can just mark that building as a waypoint in the mapping software and upload it to the GPS device. Then we can use GPS to navigate directly overland to the building, and you guys can skip all this ridiculous underground maze-running nonsense."

With a few more taps and clicks, Cyril scrolls the satellite image, looking for the cave. Then Jake squints at the screen and says, "That's the outcropping, isn't it? Where the cave is?"

"Yeah, right there!" says Lucas, pointing at the screen.

Lexi nods. "I see the cave mouth," she says.

Cyril zooms the satellite view closer and sure enough, there's the now-familiar topography of the rocky outcropping, its cave mouth, and the surrounding woods. He zooms back out and then punches a button. Now Cyril's GameGeek 3-D maze-map of the Slorg's den appears as a transparent overlay on top of the satellite image. With surgical skill, Cyril aligns the air-tunnel opening seen on the actual satellite map with the Slorg cave entrance on his game map. Then he clicks to lock the two maps together.

"Bingo," he says. "We have Vulcan map meld."

"Awesome!" says Lucas.

"Now let's see where this crazy maze leads to," says Cyril.

He punches a key and a glowing red dot pops into view over the cave entrance on the map. Then Cyril hits another key. Team Spy Gear watches breathlessly as the dot slowly moves, drawing a red line along its route. The dot follows the "critical path" (gamer lingo for "most direct route to solution") that Cyril and the gang mapped through the maze yesterday to the Slorg Treasure Room.

When it finally reaches its destination, the red dot starts pulsing.

The four kids stare in confusion at the map location on the satellite image.

"That's the Carrolton Reservoir," says Jake.

Lucas turns to Cyril, frowning. He says, "Firelight Studios is . . . *underwater?*"

14

DUCT WALK

The cave mouth looks disturbingly like an actual mouth. Ferns jut over the opening like green teeth. Warm wet air blows out like stale meat-breath. Despite this, Lexi dives inside.

Lucas stares into the black hole.

"You know," he says, "once we go in, we're more or less trapped."

"And thanks for that insight," says Jake, shining a flashlight into the abyss.

Hey, funny, says Cyril via Spy Link. That's exactly what terrifies me about caves too!

Jake sighs.

Okay, so you go inside, says Cyril. Say some predator decides to follow. Now what? What are your alternatives? You have none.

"Right," says Lucas. "Basically, you're just asking to be cornered and gored."

The feeling of desperation must be gut-wrenching, says Cyril. Pinned by grim, pitiless tusks to a rock wall. Utter blackness. No hope. Nobody hears your pathetic, miserable shrieks.

Lexi pokes her head back out. "It's *awesome* in here!" she says happily.

"Lead the way," says Jake.

"Sweet!" says Lexi.

She disappears back into the cave. Jake and Lucas exchange an uneasy look.

Cyril says, Ah, Wonder Woman is back.

Lucas says, "Yeah, well, she hasn't hit the M3 Pause key in a few days. Apparently, the game's subliminal mind control programming wears off fairly quickly."

There's a pause. Then Cyril says, I wonder what it's like to be gored.

"Cyril!" says Jake, exasperated.

Lucas suddenly slings his gadget backpack to the ground. "Hey, I've got an idea!" he says.

"Lucas has an idea," reports Jake. "I repeat, *Lucas has an idea*."

Uh-oh, says Cyril.

Knowing this could take some time, Lexi reappears at the cave mouth and climbs out.

* * *

The Spy Gear Lazer Tripwire Personal Security System is an elegant thing . . . especially in the hands of a gadget artist like Lucas Bixby.

Lucas clamps a gray metallic device labeled LTW-001 on a low mulberry root near the cave mouth. "This is the master unit," he says.

Do we bow before it? asks Cyril in the Spy Link.

Lucas ignores the comment as he adjusts the clamp.

All hail the master unit! intones Cyril.

"Cyril," says Jake patiently.

"Okay, the circuit is almost complete," says Lucas.

Two secondary units, LTW-002 and LTW-003, are clamped on rock shards around the cave mouth: one high, one low. The three units form a triangle.

"See how each lazer unit has a Sender and a Receptor?" says Lucas.

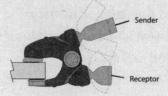

He explains how the slim, swiveling Sender scope shoots a red light beam; the rotating Receptor pod is a light sensor.

"Now, the idea is to create a circuit of connected light," explains Lucas. "You connect the units using the light beams. Isn't this the coolest thing since, like, cell phones?"

I'd have to go clear back to the garlic press, says Cyril.

Lucas delicately swivels LTW-001's Sender scope so its red light beam shines across the cave mouth directly into the Receptor sensor pod on LTW-002.

The master unit chirps a robotic message: "System . . . armed."

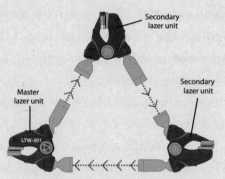

"Now, if anything big or small moves through any of these light beams," says Lucas, backing away, "it'll break the circuit and thus trigger an alarm."

"So this system will detect anything that tries to enter the cave behind us?" asks Jake.

"Correct," says Lucas, pointing at LTW-001. "The alarm siren is in that master unit."

"But how will we hear it?" asks Lexi, looking over the gadgetry.

"Good point," says Jake. "We'll be deep in the tunnels."

Lucas unzips a side pouch on his gadget backpack and pulls out a ball-shaped Spy Bug, a high-tech remote listening device. Then he flips a switch and the ball's top half flips up, revealing a dish receiver that looks like a radar base.

"This bug will pick up the alarm," says Lucas, setting it next to the LTW-001 unit. Then he pulls out the Spy Bug's receiver unit, clips it on his belt, and runs a wire with an attached earbud up to his free ear. "Then I'll hear it via this hookup."

Plus you'll have me for backup alert, says Cyril. I've got the Lazer Tripwire's alarm frequency patched into an audio channel here at HQ, too.

Lexi shakes her head in awe. "You rock," she says, pointing at Lucas.

"No, you rock," says Lucas, pointing back.

"No, you."

"You!"

"You."

"No, you."

"Nice system, bro," says Jake. "Now we can know in advance that we're trapped."

Yes, says Cyril via Spy Link. It should give you just enough time to panic.

Lucas pushes the power button on the LTW-001 unit to disable the alarm. The three explorers step into the cave mouth. Then Lucas reaches back out to re-arm the Lazer Tripwire system.

"System . . . armed," says the robotic voice.

* * *

Inside, Jake fires up a Nightwriter flashlight. He swings its cool blue oval of light from side to side.

"Interesting," he says.

The entry "cavern" is not a cave at all, but rather a circular chamber. Its walls are smooth, heavy-duty plastic. Three duct openings, each six feet high, lead into long, dark ventilation pipes. In each pipe, a dull distant hum and a light breeze indicate the presence of exhaust fans beating somewhere deeper in the system.

"Okay, guys," says Jake, his voice a hollow echo. "Got your zipper tools?"

"Roger," replies Lucas.

Lexi says, "Got mine."

"Clip and light," says Jake.

Each explorer illuminates a small but powerful Spy Gear LED Flashlight hanging on a zip-clip attached to a side zipper of their cargo pants. Bright red lights illuminate the ground.

Jake finds the cozy red glow slightly comforting. But only slightly. "Let's go," he says. "Which way, Cyril?"

Center duct, replies Cyril.

Lexi darts through the center duct opening, and the Bixby boys follow.

After nearly an hour of dead silence and inactivity, Mr. Latimer begins to wonder about the three black cars. Are they sleeping, or what?

But suddenly things happen, and they happen swiftly.

The engine of the black sedan facing Mr. Latimer roars to life. Its tires yelp as it accelerates. The sedan whizzes past his blue Avalon and squeals around a corner, heading toward Carrolton Reservoir.

Meanwhile, all four doors of the second black sedan burst open at the same time. Four men emerge from the car, one from each door. They slam their doors shut and sprint toward Stoneship Woods. Each man wears sunglasses and a dark suit.

But there's no movement from the black BMW—none whatsoever.

Mr. Latimer is torn. He wants to follow the first sedan. But something about this BMW makes him think twice. It feels like the command unit.

So Mr. Latimer stays put.

As dusk slowly falls, he keeps a sharp eye on the uninvited intruder.

Cyril's map is perfect. The route through the air pipes matches the game's maze route exactly. The only difference is that no red-eyed cave creatures attack—no Razor Rats, no Sabertooth worms, and (thank goodness) no skin-sucking squidlets.

Control, how do we get past this six-foot ventilation fan? asks Jake over the Spy Link.

Cyril taps on his laptop to bring up a solution text file.

"Uh, let's see," he says, scanning the text. "In the game, you either hack off the fan blades with a diamond-edged Rankkor Axe or else shoot the hub with a Photonic Blaster."

There's a pause. Then: Cyril?

"Yeah, Jake?"

I don't have a Rankkor Axe handy.

Cyril grins. "How fast are the blades spinning?"

Very slowly.

"Try grabbing one."

Grab a fan blade?

"Yeah," says Cyril. "Grab it."

There is a long pause. Then:

Actually, says Jake, that worked pretty good.

I'm through, says Lexi.

I'm clear, says Lucas.

"Okay, let's move on then, shall we?" Cyril scrolls his map. "Look for a side vent. It should be on the left side of the pipe, about twelve paces past the rotating fan."

Jake says, Ah. Found it.

"Slide through. That should put you in a parallel pipe, heading west." Cyril checks the solution text file again. "You guys don't see any Acid Bats hanging from the ceiling, do you?"

Nope. No bats, says Jake.

"No Helldog carcasses rising anew from the Pit of Stench?"

None.

Cyril sighs. "This is too easy," he says.

And so it goes. Within less than half an hour the three tunnel-runners reach the long but dead-straight final stretch of pipe that leads to their destination, the Slorg Treasure Room—or whatever its real-world equivalent turns out to be.

"Now this approach tunnel has a pretty dang steep downward slope," warns Cyril.

A negative inclination, right? says Jake.

"Right. Take it slow."

Out of the corner of his eye, Cyril catches movement on one of the side monitors above the command console. But when he turns to look at the surveillance feed, he sees nothing.

Control, is your game map still linked to the satellite image of the woods? asks Lucas.

"That's affirmative, Lima Bravo," says Cyril, still eyeing the side console monitor.

So you can plot our location?

"Roger. I can."

Are we at the Carrolton Reservoir yet? asks Lucas.

Cyril turns back to his laptop. "No," he says. "But you're near its shoreline now."

Down in the pipe, Jake notices strips of light hitting the floor just ahead. He approaches them and looks up. A circular vent cap is recessed into the top of the pipe. Sunlight is visible through its slats.

Lucas joins him and says, "Looks like we're right at the surface."

"I think we've been very close to the surface all along," says Jake. "My guess is that most of these ducts run just at ground level, or maybe even hump slightly aboveground in places, like here."

Lexi moves past the Bixbys, shining her LED Flashlight up ahead. At the next pipe joint, she stops.

"Here's the drop-off," she calls.

Lucas arrives next to her. He gazes down the next pipe section, which veers downward at a sharp angle. Then Jake joins them too.

"Looks like the longest playground tube-slide in recorded history," he says, beaming his blue flashlight downward.

"You think maybe this runs directly into the water of the reservoir?" asks Lucas.

"No," says Lexi.

"Why not?"

"I feel air coming up."

Lucas lifts his chin. "Ah, good point. I feel it now too."

"Must be another ventilation fan down there," says Jake. He looks from Lucas to Lexi.

"Okay," he says. "I want you two to follow me close when we—"

But before Jake can finish, Lexi is already sliding down the pipe.

Back at HQ, Cyril catches another glimpse of movement in the trees on the side monitor.

Okay, Lucas and I are ready to slide down the pipe, says Jake. Does it seem odd to you that a ventilation duct would run underneath a reservoir?

"Yes it does," chimes in Cyril. "And guys, I've got movement here on the south perimeter."

Are you locked down? asks Jake.

"Of course I'm locked down," says Cyril. "All doors shut and sealed."

Maybe it's Marco, says Lexi. The transmission of her voice crackles in the console speakers.

"Yes, that would be good," says Cyril, staring hard now at the monitor displaying the south perimeter video feed. "But this thing is in the trees. Staying out of sight."

That isn't Marco, then, says Lexi. Static nearly drowns out her voice now.

"No," says Cyril. "Probably not. Probably just something else. No big deal. Just something out there, moving around, lurking. Stalking. Whatever. I'll just forget about it and, like, whatever." He wipes sweat dripping down the bridge of his nose. "Maybe I'll bake some croissants."

A sudden beep makes Cyril yelp and nearly jump out of his chair.

He turns to the sound source. His eyes widen.

"Omega input incoming!" he says breathlessly.

Someone responds, but the reply is unintelligible due to radio static.

"Repeat, repeat, Omega input incoming," says Cyril. "Field team, do you read me?"

Static crackles in the speakers.

"Yo, guys, do you read me? Hello? Hello?"

Now, only silence. No static—nothing.

"Great," says Cyril.

He shakes his head, thinking, *I should have known.* As the field team descends deeper underground, interference naturally increases and the com-link deteriorates. Cyril turns to the Omega Link on the edge of the command console. But before he can grab it, a siren alarm shatters the silence. Cyril's squeal is so high-pitched that only cats can hear it. He looks around, embarrassed.

He swivels to the console display and checks the digital audio channel readouts.

It's the Lazer Tripwire system.

"Guys!" shouts Cyril into the console mike. "Can you hear me?"

Still no response.

"Something is entering the cave," he calls.

Now more dark movement flickers on the south video feed. Cyril stares at it.

"Things are coming," says Cyril hoarsely.

(15)

NO SUCH THING?

The notion of walking directly beneath four thousand acre-feet of reservoir water—and a quick calculation reveals its water weight to be over five million tons—is just a *little* unsettling, isn't it?

But sometimes spies have a job to do, and you just have to foolishly ignore the danger.

After dropping steeply for about forty yards, the last stretch of ventilation pipe finally levels off. A few feet farther ahead, another large ventilation fan spins lazily. But the field team has no trouble grabbing a blade and then hopping through the fan as its motor whines in complaint.

Now Lexi dashes quickly ahead.

"As I recall," says Lucas, following, "the Slorg Treasure Room is just around one final bend in the tunnel. Right, Cyril?"

Static crackles in the team's Spy Link earpieces.

"Cyril?" calls Jake.

More static.

"This is Field Team calling Mission Control, do you read me, over?"

Static. Then dead air.

"We probably lost him when we dropped deeper down the last pipe," says Lucas.

"This isn't good," says Jake, worried. "I want more reports on that south perimeter movement."

"Maybe we should go back," says Lucas.

"Let me try my cell phone," says Jake.

Lucas shakes his head. "I doubt it works down here either."

Jake flips open his phone. Sure enough, the NO SER-VICE message appears on its viewscreen.

Something clatters loudly up ahead. Then the boys hear Lexi scream.

"Lexi!" shouts Lucas as both Bixbys scramble wildly around the bend in the pipe.

Up ahead, Jake's blue flashlight beam reveals a rectangular air grate on the floor of the pipe. It's open and hanging down. Bright bluish light shines up through the opening.

"I'm okay," calls Lexi from somewhere below.

The boys reach the grate and look down to see Lexi just a few feet under them. Illuminated in blue, she stands on a huge desk littered with papers and cups. Numerous slick-looking workstations linked by network cables are arrayed around the desktop.

"*Oh, my, God,*" says Lucas in hushed awe.

Lexi grins up at him.

Lucas can barely speak. "I thought it was myth, like Valhalla," he says. "But . . . *it's real!*"

"Nobody's here," says Lexi.

Jake and Lucas exchange a look of disbelief, and then drop into the "Slorg Treasure Room" below.

Parents, let me give you a little heads-up here.

Few things hold as much fascination for a typical kid as the idea of exploring the inner sanctum of a videogame design studio. By inner sanctum, of course, we mean the Quality Assurance department—often called the "testing pit"—where game testers hammer away at games in development, looking for bugs and playing until their eyes bleed.

Most studios are places where guys with long stringy hair suck down carbonated caffeine syrup (called "energy drinks") and play extreme Ping-Pong at 4:00 a.m. because real life has no place for them. But kids don't know that. They see only hallowed ground, sanctified by the holiest of holy occupations.

Right now, for example, Lucas Bixby and Lexi Lopez gaze in awe at a logo etched in adobe on the wall: a simple line sketch of a computer monitor with a candle glowing on its screen, its flame a minimalist splash of orange and yellow.

"Firelight Studios," says Lexi in a hushed voice.

Lucas nods. "The hottest game studio in the world," he whispers.

Both gaze up at the logo with a veneration bordering on cult worship. The possibility that this might be the lair of Viper-associated bad guys running a ruthless mind-control experiment on kids is completely lost on them at first. But then Lucas looks closer at the logo.

"Lexi," he says. "Look at the flame's tip."

Both kids lean closer to the logo. The candle flame flares slightly into an unmistakable shape.

"See the forked tongue?" says Lucas.

"That's a snakehead," says Lexi.

Nearby, Jake stands looking at a very formidable-looking industrial security door. "Here's the main exit, but I wonder where it leads?" he asks aloud. He examines a glowing, five-button keypad on the door. "Looks like we need a five-digit pass code."

"To exit?" asks Lexi, who walks up next to him.

"Good point," says Jake. He tries the door, but it's locked tight. "Hmmm. Why would you need a pass code to *exit* your offices?" He glances over at Lucas. "Got any theories, bro?"

"This place is so sweet you could, like, pour it on your pancakes," replies Lucas, still mesmerized.[7]

The "Slorg Treasure Room" turns out to be a large, open office space. The center area is the Pit, where the testers "work."[8] Around it, portable dividers form dozens of standard office cubicles. Overall, the place looks like any corporate cube-city, except for the wild variety of wacky stuff cluttering desks—including numerous plastic toy models of familiar monsters from The Massively Multiplayer Mystery.

"That's a Bogassian Pit Beetle, isn't it?" says Lucas, pointing at a huge bug with a chainsaw.

"Yes," says Lexi.

"There's a Phlegm Spider. Sick!"

"But where is everybody?" asks Jake, picking up a half-full can of root beer. "And what's with the blue lighting?"

"It is eerie," admits Lucas.

Lexi moves across the room, exploring further.

"People just walked out," says Jake. Still carrying the root beer, he notes jackets hung on chairs clustered around a conference table. Then he notices several pairs

---

7. This is an old saying Lucas picked up from Mrs. Bixby, who in turn got it from her own mom, and so on back through history, mom to mom, almost a thousand years to its origin with William the Conqueror's mom, who spoke it on the field of battle at Hastings while swinging her long-sword (which, coincidentally, she had named "Bixby") at Anglo-Saxons, a historical moment that also forms the origin of the phrase, "Yeah, your *mom* fights Anglo-Saxons."

8. Ha! Right.

of shoes on the floor. "Or maybe *ran* out," he adds. "Like, in a big hurry."

Lucas says, "This reminds me of when we first found Stoneship."

Indeed, there are resemblances. Stuff is lying around as if abandoned in mid-meeting. But this place is much more *recently* abandoned than Stoneship. In fact, the root beer can is still cold.

Jake sets it down, feeling spooked.

Nearby, Lucas notices an open closetlike room. Inside, a big workstation hums. As he approaches, he sees a bright red line on the floor across the doorway. A sign on the outside of the open door reads DO NOT ENTER! AUTHORIZED ACCESS ONLY! in big red letters.

Naturally, Lucas enters. Hey, the door's open, right? According to kid rules, he has no choice. He sees a central monitor. Onscreen, a big software logo reads:

Serpentine BH-Mod 6.3
Pass: _____

"Jake!" calls Lucas.

Jake enters the alcove. He reads the screen aloud: "BH-Mod." He looks at Lucas.

There is a pause.

"Behavior modification," say the Bixbys in unison.

"Holy monkfish," says Lucas uneasily. "They must program their subliminal mind-whacking stuff on this." He poises unsteady fingers over the workstation's keyboard. "Any ideas on a password?"

"No clue," says Jake, picking up a yellow sheet of notebook paper ripped out of a notebook. Messy handwritten notes cover the page. At the top, a list is printed in large capital letters:

PHASE 1: COOPERATIVE
PHASE 2: TRIBAL
PHASE 3: HOSTILE
PHASE 4: HERO/SAVIOR

"Good gosh," says Jake. As Lucas looks over his shoulder, Jake reads aloud a note scrawled in a corner: "Phase 4: After S spurs clan wars, enter NPC Warrior Hero. WH kills S. All clans hail, submit, consolidate. Security. Rule of WH. Name?"

"What's it mean?" asks Lucas.

The boys study the scribbled notes, which make clear that Firelight plans a game narrative where the "S"—the Slorg, no doubt—wreaks havoc in the M3 universe. Clans get scared, blame each other, and start fighting. Then Firelight introduces a studio-controlled hero/savior to offer security and leadership.

Lucas looks at his brother. "What a lame story line," he says.

"Yes," says Jake. "But what a great test of mass mind control." A chill runs up his spine. "These guys are using a computer game to test basic fear-triggers on people. And they're doing this to modify the *real-world* behavior of their game subscribers!"

"Only a real *snake* would try something like that," agrees Lucas.

"What's this noise?" calls Lexi, who has her ear to a door across the room.

Jake sets down the note page and the boys join Lexi at the door. Its sign reads BREEDING CHAMBERS.

Lucas says, "This must be the creature design area, where the studio's artists and 3D modelers create all the weird monsters for the games." He points at the sign. "Game designers crack me up."

"But what's that sound?" asks Lexi again.

They all listen quietly. A low hum can be heard on the other side of the door. It has an odd quality to it—mechanical, yet somehow different, too.

"Aha!" says Lucas.

A rapt look comes over his face. Jake and Lexi watch him, waiting.

"The servers!" he finally says.

"What?"

"The universe servers," says Lucas. "The large mega-capacity computer servers where M3 actually exists! Where the game world lives and breathes! Where thousands and thousands of avatars like Ralph the Mighty rise each day to walk the land!"

Jake squints at him. "A little melodramatic there, sport," he says.

"But it's true!"

Lexi nods in awe too. "Can we see them?"

Lucas stares at her. "Dare we?"

Jake rolls his eyes, but says, "Okay, let's check it out." He opens the door. The odd hum grows louder. He peeks inside.

Perplexed, he asks, "What is this?"

Lucas peers in too. "What the monkey?"

The three kids step into a large laboratory, blue-lit and gleaming. Work desks covered with very scientific-looking instrumentation run along three of the room's walls. Up on the ceiling a large circular spout or nozzle gleams silver-blue in the light.

The far wall, opposite the doorway, is lined with cylindrical glass chambers, each about four feet tall and bathed in blue light. The chambers rise up from humming consoles with colorful flashing lights and glowing digital readouts.

From across the room, these glass chambers appear to be filled with swirling blue mist. But a closer examination reveals the "mist" to be tiny moving particles. And still closer inspection reveals these particles to be something that Lucas finds most alarming.

"Bugs!" he cries.

* * *

Mr. Latimer sees the woods shaking before he actually hears the rotor blades; that's how quickly and quietly the black helicopter arrives on the scene.

Sitting up in his Avalon, he raises a Spy Night Scope (courtesy of Lucas Bixby, weeks ago) to his eyes and watches the craft drift over the tree line, then stop and hover.

After a few seconds, a cargo hatch opens on the underside of its black carapace. Then a large container drops from the hatch on a winch line. It is slowly lowered into the trees.

Yes, each glass cylinder in the blue-lit lab contains a different breed of insect. One holds mosquitoes. Another is full of flies. Still another is crawling with zillions of tiny centipedes. A total of ten bug-filled chambers line the wall. Above each is a large monitor.

"Why in the name of human sanity would a flipping videogame company breed bugs?" asks Lucas, backing away from the chambers in horror. His breath feels a little short and huffy.

"Careful there," says Jake.

Lucas backs into a workstation with a large display screen. The heel of his hand hits a keyboard. Something beeps. He turns and looks at the screen.

A window opens that reads CHAMBER LIST. Underneath it is an onscreen button icon that reads OPEN.

Instinctively, Lucas grabs the workstation mouse and clicks on OPEN.

Sure enough, a file list opens. Ten file icons appear, designated by letter—Chamber A, Chamber B, Chamber C, and so on—plus two files listed apart from the others at the bottom, named Master Chamber I and Master Chamber II. Each chamber name on the screen has another OPEN button next to it.

"Yo, check this out," he calls to the others.

Jake and Lexi join him at the workstation screen.

Lucas quickly clicks on the OPEN button next to Chamber A. An information window pops open. It lists the following data:

SPECIES	**Aedus AP 3.2**
GEN-MOD	**Yes**
GENERATION	**581**
CHAR/TRAIT	**Aggressive**

"Aedus AP," says Lucas, pointing. "That would be *Aedus albopictus*, better known as the Asian tiger mosquito. Or some variant, anyway. I don't know what the three-point-two designation means."

Lexi looks at him. "You *know* that?"

Lucas clicks on another link. "Everybody knows that."

"Really?"

"Aedus is one of the three most common mosquito

species in the United States. It's associated with the transmission of dengue fever, eastern equine encephalitis, and heartworm."

Even Jake, who is rarely surprised by his brothers insane curiosity about things, has to raise his eyebrows at this info. "Wow."

"Wow is right."

Jake looks at the screen. "That sounds like nasty stuff."

"It is," says Lucas.

Lucas scans some very scientific-looking info that pops up onscreen. "Hmmm," he says. "I'm not sure, but this Chamber A data seems to be derived from some sort of genetic modification experiment."

"You think that's what 'GEN-MOD' means?" says Jake, pointing at the screen.

"Yep."

Lexi glances over at the first chamber across the room. The console beneath it is marked with the letter A. "Why would Firelight Studios be messing with mosquitoes?" she asks.

"I don't know," says Jake.

Lucas continues his scan of the bug files. He reads data on some of the other chambers. The centipedes are a mutation of the species *Scolopendra*, bred for speed, aggression, and their tiny size. The flies are *Simulium arcticum*, the dreaded biting black fly, well known for its swarming and persistent attacks. In fact, all of these chambered species seem to share aggressive, attacking traits.

Suddenly a telephone rings loudly. All three kids jump and yell.

After a second ring, an answering machine takes the call. "You've reached the Firelight Studios answering machine. Please leave a message and we'll—" But the caller hangs up.

Lucas, recovering from the jolt, turns to look at Jake. "A phone answering machine?" he says. "Gee, that's pretty low-tech for such a high-tech place."

Jake's eyes suddenly widen. "A land line!" he says.

Lucas frowns, not getting it.

Jake hustles to the phone, picks up the receiver, and starts punching in a number.

When Cyril's cell phone rings, he's in the process of piling every loose object in Stoneship HQ on top of the entry hatch on the floor. Chairs. A shelf. Two unattached monitors. A fax machine. Coffee cups. Anything to add weight. It's a pathetic attempt, of course. But Cyril is a man possessed.

The reason for this frenetic activity is the latest Omega Link message, a simple command:

DO NOT OPEN MASTER II

When Cyril read this a minute ago, the meaning seemed clear. Something lurks in the now-darkening woods south of Stoneship. Maintain master lockdown! Cyril remembers how back in Book One (see, even Cyril has read it) a dark intruder cut power to the entire warehouse and managed to open the entry hatch. So now Cyril is piling stuff on top of it. Empty CD cases. Pens. Crumpled paper. His shoes. Socks.

Now Cyril looks at the incoming caller info on his cell phone's display. It says CALL BLOCKED.

He answers anyway.

"Who is this?" he yells.

"Dude, ouch, says the voice. My ear. Dog, that hurts."

"Jake?" yells Cyril. "Jake?"

"Yes, and please stop."

"Where are you?" says Cyril, hurrying to the plate-glass window overlooking the warehouse floor. "Who's following you?"

"What? Nobody," answers Jake. "Hey, you won't believe it. We're inside Firelight Studios! For real!"

"No way!"

"But here's what's whacked. We found a room full of insects."

Cyril frowns. "Insects?"

"Right. Big containers. Somebody is breeding bugs. But we don't know why yet."

"Jake," says Cyril.

"Yes?"

"Somebody's following you."

"What? How do you know?"

"The Lazer Tripwire alarm went off about ten minutes ago."

There's a pause. Then: "Guys, Cyril thinks someone else is in the tunnels."

As Jake chats with Cyril, Lucas turns his attention to the two files labeled Master Chamber. As Lexi watches over his shoulder, he clicks open Master Chamber I. Under another bio-data screen, a rotating 3D model of a black beast pops onscreen.

"The Slorg?" says Lucas.

He turns to Lexi. She just stares at the screen.

"It's *real*," she says.

"No, there's no such thing," says Lucas.

He scans the screen again. Next to the bio-data window sits a small icon labeled OBS-Cams. He clicks it and four video windows appear.

"Those are live feeds," says Lucas. "Looks like four different angles of the same holding chamber." He looks at Lexi again. "Observation cameras."

"What are they observing?" asks Lexi.

The chamber is empty. Lucas looks at it and says, "I

don't know. The subject is gone." He looks up at Lexi. "Escaped, maybe."

"It's the Slorg pen, isn't it?" says Lexi.

Lucas, eyeing the data window, says, "You know, this bio-data is, uh, very *actual* looking."

Jake, still on the phone with Cyril, calls out, "Guys, we really need to get out of here. The Lazer Tripwire went off a while ago."

"Okay, okay," calls back Lucas. "Let me check just one more thing."

He clicks back to the main screen to check out the Master Chamber II file. As he clicks on its OPEN button, he hears Jake say, "Another Omega message? What's it say, Cyril?"

The Master Chamber II data window opens. It is blank.

Next to this window is another OPEN icon. Lucas clicks on it.

Just then he hears Jake say, "Do not open master two. Huh." Jake glances over at Lucas. "Bro, does the message 'Do not open master two' mean anything to you?"

Lucas looks at the screen, feeling sick.

"Maybe," he says.

Loud mechanical clicks, whines, and whirrs begin to echo in the wall behind the row of glass chambers. Then a buzzing begins to build in intensity.

On the display screen, a new message flashes in red letters.

It reads:

CHAMBER BREECH EMERGENCY DETECTED

"Uh-oh," says Lucas.

He looks up. The buzzing grows louder. Then, in the muted blue light, he sees what appears to be an oil slick creeping slowly across the walls and ceiling from behind the glass chambers.

Finally, movement from the black BMW!

The Beemer's driver-side door opens and a dark figure steps out.

Mr. Latimer resists the urge to applaud.

Over the trees, he can still see the ghostly black helicopter and hear the strangely muted thrumming of its rotor blades.

The dark man—for indeed, it is the Dark Man, as you no doubt guessed a couple of days ago—hobbles slowly into the woods.

He only trips once.

Cyril says, "What do you mean, stuff on the walls? Jake? Jake?" He holds up his cell phone. "He hung up on me."

Then the Omega Link beeps again. Cyril grabs the device and reads a new message:

FS DOOR CODE 2219X
CLOSE DOOR BEHIND YOU

"Door code?" says Cyril. "FS?" He thinks for a moment, and then says, "Ah, Firelight Studios." He opens his cell phone, but remembers that only CALL BLOCKED appeared on the Caller ID display when Jake phoned him, so he has no callback number.

"Great," he says, staring at his phone. "Jake, I've got a door code for you, but you *just won't listen.*"

Cyril glances out the control room window again. He notices that something *very* interesting is happening below in the warehouse.

The south door is opening.

"Oh this is perfect," he says. "What a great *lockdown* we have here."

Cyril ducks down out of sight, looking around desperately for a weapon of defense. Unfortunately, the best he can come up with is a stapler.

"Yes!" he whispers, grabbing it. "Bring it on!"

Cyril turns to face the floor hatch, which is piled up so heavily that surely no creature could penetrate such a barricade.

The hatch slowly slides open.

The chair on the bottom that supports the whole pile cracks loudly and breaks. All of the stuff falls straight through the hole, shattering in great cacophony on the floor down below.

Cyril grimaces.

"Okay," he says. "So I'm an idiot."

Wielding the stapler, he approaches the now-open hatch. With a shaky voice, he calls out, "Hey! Hey! Who's down there?"

No answer.

Cyril drops to his knees, pulls open the stapler, and holds it over the brink of the open hatch.

Hysterically, he shouts, "Yo, jack, you want some of *this* bad boy?"

Lucas is paralyzed by fear.

For it is clear that somewhere behind the far wall, a massive vat of wall-crawling insects has just been unleashed. And now the black swarm advances over the room. The blue lighting reflects in a deep velvet-black glimmer on their exoskeletons.

"Let's go!" shouts Jake, who slams down the phone and grabs Lexi's arm. "Lucas, out of the room! Now!"

Lucas backs a step away from the console display. But then another message window appears onscreen. It reads:

CONTINGENCY PLAN A
OPEN

Lucas stares at it for a second as the odd buzzing and the hushed skittering of spiky legs moves across the walls toward him. Then he impulsively reaches for the mouse and clicks on the OPEN button.

Now a very loud siren starts blaring. Lucas covers his ears as the shriek pierces his skull. One of the glass chambers shatters and mosquitoes pour out. A last message window pops onscreen:

PLAN A ACTIVE
EVACUATE

"Lucas!" shouts Jake. He rushes up and grabs his brother by the arm. Mosquitoes buzz around their heads.

Above them, the circular spout in the ceiling starts to drone and whine. Water starts to dribble through the spout as its iris-like nozzle slowly opens. Within seconds, the water jet increases in pressure, shooting a hard white stream straight down at the floor.

"That must be the reservoir!" shouts Jake over the growing roar.

Swatting at mosquitoes, he drags Lucas through the open door and slams it shut. Lexi waits in the office area. She looks wide-eyed and, frankly, exhilarated.

"That door won't hold," she says, and dang it, she just can't help it: She smiles.

"I'm sure you're right," says Jake. "Let's climb back up into the ventilation duct. We'll retrace our route to the cave opening. Cyril can guide us once we get closer to the surface and into Spy Link contact."

"Wait a minute!" says Lucas. "Didn't Cyril tell you somebody followed us into the caves?"

"We'll have to tackle that problem when we come to it," says Jake.

The dull roar of the water jet in the next room gets louder, and water begins seeping under the door. As the water pressure on the door grows, it creaks and groans.

"To the duct!" orders Jake.

The three spies hustle to the hanging grate and climb easily back up into the ceiling duct. Across the room, the Breeding Chamber door bursts open. Water gushes out in a three-foot wave.

"Once we get up the steep pipe, we're above water level, so we'll be fine," says Jake, shepherding Lucas along the duct. Lexi scrambles up ahead. "Stay close!" calls Jake to her. "We don't know what's up there yet." He fires up his flashlight and then pats Lucas. "You okay, bub?"

"A vat of mutant killer fire ants, or whatever those were," says Lucas, trembling as he moves along. "Wow. I guess that's one good reason to build a secret laboratory directly underneath a city reservoir."

As they reach the top of the sloped pipe, Jake starts calling to Cyril via Spy Link. Cyril immediately answers: I read you, field team.

"Hey, man!" says Jake, happy to hear that voice again. "We, like, flooded out the lab and all the bugs and stuff. It was nuts, I tell you."

Where are you? asks Cyril quickly.

"Just climbed back up the sloped pipe," says Jake. "Heading back to the exit now."

You can't, says Cyril.

Jake frowns. "Why not?"

Because they sealed off the cave.

"What?! Who did?"

Some guys with a black helicopter.

Jake takes a breath. "How do you know that?"

I just watched them do it.

"From HQ?"

No, dude, says Cyril. I'm in the woods.

Jake turns to Lucas, who looks ill. Lucas points to his ear with the Spy Bug receiver.

"I hear them," says Lucas. "Jake! I hear it. We're trapped in here!"

No you're not, says Cyril calmly. Listen, guys. Do you remember that ceiling thingy you mentioned before, where you could see sunlight? You should be near it now, right? Top of the sloped pipe?

"Right," says Jake. He raises his flashlight to the ceiling. He moves down the pipe a few paces, then spots the vent cap. "Here it is," he says.

Excellent! says Cyril. Now get away from it.

"What?"

Step away from it.

"Okay."

Jake and the others back down the tunnel.

Suddenly the vent makes two loud cracking sounds. The third time, the plastic cap shatters. Pieces clatter to the pipe floor.

"Hand me a kid!" growls a voice from above.

"Marco!" cries Lexi.

"*Woo-hoo!*" cheers Lucas.

The Bixbys boost Lexi up to the hole, where Marco's big hairy hands grab her and yank her out. As Jake cups his hands to boost Lucas next, the boys hear a loud snorting sound just up the pipe.

Lucas freezes. He whispers, "Slorg!"

"There's no such thing," says Jake.

"Yes there is!" whispers Lucas.

Another snort! Jake hefts his brother upward with superhuman vigor. Then, as he reaches up to clasp Marco's hands, a rasping breath approaches rapidly down the tunnel. He can hear the scraping clatter of talons on the plastic pipe floor.

"Pull!" he yells to Marco. "Pull!"

The black helicopter still hovers above the woods, but it circles now, shining its bright greenish spotlight into the trees. After a few minutes, however, it swivels its nose toward Carrolton Reservoir and zooms with remarkable speed into the darkness.

Night has fully fallen now.

Mr. Latimer watches the woods intently with his Spy Night Scope.

Nothing is moving.

Then Mr. Latimer decides to take a rare chance. He exits his Avalon and strolls very casually up the road toward the BMW. When he reaches the German car, he looks around and listens.

All is quiet.

Then he flicks on his Spy Pen flashlight and aims the beam through the passenger-side window of the BMW. The glass is tinted, but he can still see a black briefcase on the leather seat.

Lying on top of the briefcase is a large, glossy eight-by-ten photograph.

It appears to be some sort of black beast. It has a snout. It looks familiar. Mr. Latimer remembers seeing this thing.

What is it?

Why is the Dark Man tracking it?

What's going on out there in Stoneship Woods?

"Whatever it is, it's *not* human," pants Lucas as he runs through a briar patch. "*Ouch!*"

Marco trots in the lead, carrying the spade he used to

smash the vent cap. "Keep running," he says. "We'll cut through the cottonwood clearing."

"But that puts us out in the open," calls Jake, who brings up the rear.

"Exactly," says Marco.

All Team Spy Gear members have switched off their Spy Link base units because they're all within earshot now. Cyril stumbles along just ahead of Jake. He reaches back and the two buddies slap hands.

"So how are you, Pizarro?" asks Cyril.

"Amazed and phenomenally relieved."

Cyril manages a weak chuckle.

"How did you find the vent cap?" asks Jake.

Cyril holds up something dark. Jake's bouncing flashlight beam hits it: the GPS receiver.

"I plotted it as a waypoint on the map overlay," says Cyril, breathing hard. "Whew! Then we downloaded it into the receiver. This GPS is amazing stuff, my man."

Up ahead, Marco bursts through a stand of saplings into an open space. Lexi and Lucas follow close behind; then the older boys enter the clearing. As Jake pushes through the tall grass, he hears it behind them: snapping branches, snarling breath.

"It's coming!" he shouts.

The team bursts into a full sprint across the open meadow. Behind, the pursuer closes swiftly. Jake refuses to look back yet. He stays behind Cyril, who flounders along like a squid doing cartwheels. Up ahead, Marco's flashlight reveals the trees on the far edge of the clearing. Beyond that, he knows, is the old access road, which stretches for another hundred yards or so until reaching the edge of the woods.

We're not gonna make it! thinks Jake.

Behind him, very close now, the horrible rasping gets louder and clearer. However, Jake notices a strange quality to the heaving breath. Instinctively, Jake senses . . . fear. Yes, that's it. It's afraid! The beast is almost on Jake's heels, but on a weird instinct . . . Jake slows down.

Behind him, the panting creature slows down too.

Jake slows to a walk.

Behind him, the creature, whatever it is, halts its pursuit.

Jake keeps walking to the tree line, but then he stops too.

He turns around.

In the center of the clearing, the dark silhouette crouches. Its glowing red eyes look to the sky. Jake is about to turn his blue flashlight beam on it. But then, up high, he hears an approaching whine. It sounds like a jet engine, but quieter and deeper. Soon he sees a circle of lights hover over the clearing. The craft drops lower, and the grass begins to whip wildly as the engine whine gets louder.

"That's no helicopter," whispers Jake, wide-eyed.

Out in the clearing, the creature looks agitated. But it does not move.

And then the spotlight, bright red, bright as a nova, blazes into the clearing. Jake is blinded. He tries to shield his eyes. All he can tell is that the craft is dropping lower and lower.

Then it rises. And in an instant, it is gone!

"Jake! Jake!" calls Lucas from afar.

"Yo, dude!" cries Cyril in the distance. "Did you see *that*?"

Jake staggers out into the clearing. As his eyes readjust to darkness, he aims his flashlight where the creature had stood.

It is gone too.

(16)

TRICK OR TREAT

Halloween is Mrs. Bixby's favorite night. It used to be Jake's, too. But the Moms of Carrolton are taking their festive hysteria to unhealthy levels. Let's face it: Kid costumes are getting out of hand.

The doorbell rings.

"Oh, look!" shrieks Mrs. Bixby with deeply massive and powerful delight. "Jake, it's Tooty the Train!"

Jake comes to the doorway carrying the candy bowl. He takes a deep breath, then peers around Mrs. Bixby.

Sure enough, on the porch stands a kid in a Tooty the Train locomotive costume, made of Kevlar and other space-age alloys, with working lights, horn, and a two-stroke steam engine. Attached to Tooty's coupler hook is a string of seventeen other kids dressed as various vintage railcars, including an open-top coal hopper, some freight boxcars, Pullman sleepers, and a caboose with a live monkey riding in a conductor costume.

Out on the sidewalk, dozens of parents with cameras shout instructions to the train. Dads dive and roll over bushes to get better photo angles.

Mrs. Bixby snaps a photo too. The camera flash blinds Tooty, who holds out his sack in the direction of the mailbox and says, "Trick or treat. My God, I can't see a thing."

Jake drops candy in Tooty's sack and does the same for each railcar that chugs sullenly past. Some of the kids try to smile. Some just sob. As the train's tail end finally approaches, Jake notices Cyril chatting with the caboose.

"I really like your marmoset," says Cyril, pointing at the monkey.

"It's a monkey," says the caboose kid.

"Marmosets are pretty easy to train, I guess," says Cyril.

"It's a *monkey*," says the caboose kid.

"Okay," says Cyril. "Well, good luck with that marmoset."

The caboose kid lunges for Cyril's throat just as Jake chucks candy into his bag. But the rest of the train yanks the caboose in a quick half arc and drags him away down the sidewalk. The monkey shrieks back at Cyril.

"No, *you're* ugly!" replies Cyril, pointing at it.

Jake grins. "Having fun?"

"Oh yeah," says Cyril. "I love Halloween." He nods at Jake. "You ready to head out?"

"Yeah, let's scoot."

"Where's your costume?"

Jake looks down at his clothes. "This *is* my costume."

Cyril nods wisely. "Going undercover."

"That's right." Jake says, grinning. "I'm a spy. We don't draw attention to ourselves."

"Got it."

Jake points at Cyril's red cloak. "What are you?"

"I'm a Red Cloak."

Jake grins. "Excellent!" They slap hands.

Suddenly, Lucas Bixby and Lexi Lopez both sprint up the front walk.

"Yo, dudes," calls Lucas breathlessly, holding up a pack of photos. "I got visuals. And they will, like, totally freak you out."

Jake and Cyril exchange an excited look.

"Upstairs," says Jake.

Team Spy Gear scrambles up the Bixby staircase, heading to the brothers' bedroom.

The Spy Zoom Cam is a pair of binoculars with a built-in 35mm telephoto camera for long-range photos. Last night, during the Stoneship Woods hubbub, Lucas managed to whip it out of his gadget backpack and snap some shots of the airship.

"The lighting's pretty poor," he says, spreading the photos across the floor. "But look at this." He plucks one photo out of the batch. "Can anybody tell me what that is?"

A hush falls over the team.

After a few seconds, Jake shakes his head. "No clue," he says.

"But it's definitely *not* a helicopter," says Lucas.

"No, definitely not."

The photo, taken while the airship was higher in the sky, shows a silhouette of its underside. Multicolored landing lights ring the bottom edge of a very circular-looking craft.

"Look at the outline," says Lucas, pointing. "It's pretty murky, but do you see any wings or rotors or, well, *anything* conventional?"

Cyril leans in close to the photo. "No, and that is just spooky," he says.

"And check out this angle!" says Lucas, sliding another photo out of the batch. "I got this shot just before the red spotlight blitzed out everything."

The dark craft is lower in the second photo, so the view is more from the side. Now its silhouette appears very slim, almost cigar-shaped.

Jake frowns. "When I saw it last night, my first thought was, you know, some Harrier-type jump-jet, with VTOL," he says. He points at the picture. "But this is just bizarre. It's *round!*"

"What's VTOL?" asks Lexi.

"Vertical Takeoff and Landing," explains Lucas.

Lexi nods. She looks closer at the photo. Then she says, "It's a flying saucer."

Cyril laughs nervously and says, "There's *no such thing*, little girl."

Lucas glances at Jake and says, "Yeah, well. I've heard *that* phrase before."

"Speaking of," says Jake, "did you get any shots of our beast-dude in the field?"

"None," says Lucas.

"Too bad," says Jake. "You know, I got the feeling it was *following* us, but not necessarily *chasing* us." He looks at Cyril. "This may shock you, man, but I'm not so afraid of it now, for some reason."

"Do you think we'll see it again?" asks Lucas.

Cyril says, "Gee, I really hope so."

Jake stares hard at the photos on the floor.

"So what is going on here?" he asks quietly. He looks up at the others, who all appear a little uneasy and yet exhilarated at the same time. Mysteries are like that. They make you scared *and* excited. You want knowledge, but you're afraid of what it might be. If you have good spy stuff, you can observe, gather data, and find out what's going on. But it's still scary to learn that, say, genetically modified snout-beasts are lurking in your town's woods and UFOs are dropping from the skies to pick them up.

"Well," says Cyril after a long silence, "this is some fine grist for my blog."

Jake grins. "You started a blog?"

First Cyril nods, then his hair nods. "Yes," he says. "I call it Cyril's Blog. You can find it at www.cyrilsblog.com." Cyril stops nodding, although the hair continues to nod a few more seconds. "As you well know, I have a lot to say, Jake."

Jake reaches out. They punch fists.

"Dog," says Jake.

"Dog," replies Cyril.

Downstairs, the doorbell rings again.

"Boys!" calls Mrs. Bixby from the front foyer below. "Come work the front door for me, okay? I'm making dinner for later."

"Coming!" reply the Bixby brothers in unison.

Lucas and Jake toss lollipops into open, outstretched sacks and say over and over, "Have a good night!" They note that most Carrolton kids seem fairly normal again. Good, healthy doses of bickering and other old-fashioned kid behavior mix in with the usual Halloween fun. Whew! It's refreshing to see.

Mr. Bixby, a tall athletic man, strolls into the front foyer with a cell phone to his ear.

"I don't like it, Chad," he says to the phone. "The contingencies are too risky. Let's rethink this."

"Hey, Dad," says Jake.

"Hi, son," says Mr. Bixby. "Say, what's going on out here? Why does the doorbell keep ringing?"

"It's Halloween."

"Really?"

The doorbell rings. Jake opens the door.

"Trick or treat!" shriek kids like a pack of ravenous wildcats. Out on the sidewalk, mothers with camcorders jostle aggressively for position.

First up is a small girl in a round, bowl-shaped slab of papier-mâché perforated with hundreds of holes.

Mr. Bixby frowns down at her. "What *are* you?" he asks.

"I'm a colander," says the small child.

"That's so *cute!*" squeals Mrs. Bixby from the kitchen.

"It's terrifying," says Mr. Bixby. He speaks into his phone: "Chad, I can't talk. I've got salad utensils approaching my porch."

"Here, Dad," says Jake, handing Mr. Bixby the candy bowl.

"What's this?"

"Candy."

Mr. Bixby looks at it.

"You can do it, Dad," says Lucas, patting him on the back. "We're heading out now."

Mr. Bixby sighs. "Okay. Have fun, kids."

"We will."

"Don't do anything illegal unless you're pretty sure you won't get caught."

"Good advice, Dad. Thanks."

"If you do have to flee the authorities," adds Mr. Bixby, "be sure to use the side door by the garage."

Jake grins. He gives Mr. Bixby a quick hug, then heads out into the haunted night.

Team Spy Gear wades through a squadron of little kids dressed as raccoons, or maybe it's a bunch of real raccoons, it's hard to tell. After working Agincourt Drive, the team veers up Willow. As they pass the schoolyard, a huge, hunched beast with massive shoulders steps out of the darkness.

"Hey, old man," says Jake, grinning.

Marco falls in silently beside them, lumbering along the street, his huge backpack clanking.

"Nice costume," says Cyril, eyeing Marco's wild thatch of dreadlocks. "*Attack of the Snakeheads* is one of my favorite movies."

Marco ignores him. They continue down the street a while, then he jabs out a hand toward Cyril.

"Here," he says.

"What's this?" asks Cyril, reaching out.

"Your *stuff*," says Marco. "I stole it."

He drops Stoneship's remote door opener into Cyril's hand.

"Cool," says Cyril, pocketing it.

Lucas looks up at Marco. "So you checked out the cave mouth?" he asks.

"Yep."

The others gaze at Marco, waiting.

He looks around. "They sealed it with some kind of rubberized bonding material, then packed in dirt and rock. Unless you get up real close, you'd never know a cave existed."

"Wow."

Marco nods. "They're good." He frowns. "I don't get why they're letting a bunch of little kids get so involved in this business."

"Exactly!" exclaims Cyril. "We're *little kids*! As I've repeatedly asked my colleagues here, why are *we* doing all the heavy lifting?"

"Well, that's the big mystery," says Jake.

"And all that *Beowulf* stuff from the Omega Link," adds Lucas. "What's up with that?"

Marco snorts. "Whoever's passing clues to you is an idiot, or a genius. Or both." He glances across the street, where two kids dressed as M3 Slorgs slink down the sidewalk. "And Firelight Studios was a front operation," he adds.

"Yeah, but for what?" asks Jake.

Marco laughs. "Take a guess," he says.

"Viper, obviously," says Jake.

Marco nods. "I think it was one of his regional operations centers."

Jake looks stunned. "He has more than one?"

"He's big," says Marco, stopping under a streetlight. "And he's deadly."

The others stop too. Up above, jagged October

clouds creep across a sickly half moon. Whispers of coming winter moan through the willows lining the street. Everybody gets a chill.

Jake looks around and says, "We've gone over Viper stuff a million times since yesterday. He tries to wreak havoc by crashing the Internet. He designs a game with fear-triggers to make people paranoid. He breeds attack bugs and possibly bioengineers bigger, more frightening creatures." Jake looks up at Marco. "Why?"

More wind hisses through trees. Somebody laughs like a lunatic just up the street.

"He has a master plan," says Marco.

"What is it?"

"I'm not sure yet."

Lucas looks forlorn. "The Firelight computer servers probably had *tons* of good data." He folds his arms tightly across his chest. "And I flushed it all away."

"No, I don't think so," says Marco.

Lucas looks at him. "What about all the experimental data in that insect lab?"

"Listen," says Marco. "Viper's too smart. Any data he left behind was left behind on purpose."

"What do you mean?" asks Jake.

Marco reaches in his pocket and pulls out a piece of paper. He hands it to Jake, who puts a flashlight beam on it. It's a printed e-mail note, and one line is highlighted in yellow.

"Viper sent me this a couple of months ago," says Marco. "Read the yellow part. The rest is just hacker logistics."

Jake reads aloud the highlighted line: "'If you make people afraid, you can get them to do anything.'"

Marco lowers his voice. He says, "That summarizes Viper's methods in a nutshell."

Cyril leans over Jake to read the quote. He says, "That's nasty."

"Yes, it is," says Marco.

Even in the lamplight, Lucas looks pale. He swallows a lump of panic and says, "So you're saying Viper would actually unleash massive swarms of mutant killer insects and stuff, like, just to *scare* people?"

Marco merely looks at him.

Witches float by on ghastly broomsticks. Grim ghouls cackle in the park, seeking the blood nourishment of children. Up on Old Cemetery Hill, dismal lights flicker as a decaying hand, its liquefying flesh dripping away like candle wax, thrusts upward and yeah, okay, maybe we're getting a little carried away with the Halloween thing, but all this Viper talk would give anyone the creeps, that's for sure.

"So the black-suited helicopter dudes are trying to stop Viper," says Jake, as everyone finally starts walking again.

"Looks that way," says Marco.

"So we're on the same side, them and us."

Marco scoffs. "I wouldn't be so sure about that."

"Well," says Lucas, "I think the black suits sealed the cave to trap the Slorg and not us."

"And that's why the beast was so scared," says Jake, nodding.

Cyril says, "Yeah, remember, the Omega Link sent us the Firelight door code so you could get out of there."

"Right," says Jake. "Maybe they just wanted us out of the way at that point."

"But whose side is the *Omega Link* on?" asks Lucas with passion. "And what about that amazing UFO airship? What is it and whose side is *it* on? It picked up the Slorg, so is it Viper's spaceship?" He shakes his head. "I mean, is Viper an alien from the Crab Nebula or something?"

Jake grins and says, "Wicked-tight questions, dude."

Lexi tugs on her costume. She's dressed as William the Conqueror's mom. "It's a mystery," she says.

Marco gives her a half smile. "Yes," he says. "That's exactly what it is."

Now Cyril grabs the Viper e-mail from Jake and rereads it: "'If you make people afraid, you can get them to do anything.'" He thinks for a second. "You know," he says, "this quote describes the Wolf Pack's insurgency tactics *perfectly*."

Jake Bixby stops in his tracks.

He looks over at his brother and says, "The Platte Park playground! Dude, I totally forgot about Brill's Halloween ambush plans!"

Lucas grins. "Well, I didn't," he says.

He pulls the Spy Zoom Cam from his gadget backpack. "I've got some sweet ideas," he says.

"Excellent!"

Marco shifts his own huge backpack higher on his shoulders. He says, "Kiddies, I'm out. I'm crashing with one of my homeys tonight. I'm sick of the woods." He shakes his snaky hair and adds, "I gotta find a job."

Jake steps toward him. "Marco?"

"Yeah?"

Jake sticks out his hand. "Thanks, man."

Marco looks at Jake's hand for a second. Then he gives it a quick shake.

"You guys got any extra popcorn balls?" he asks. "I haven't eaten in like, days."

Four treat bags open up simultaneously.

And now the satellite camera view pulls back from happy Carrolton—back, back. Team Spy Gear shrinks, as does their hungry, hairy consultant. All around, kids in costumes run from house to house. Many parents—*battalions* of parents—escort the little ones as they scurry under the warm yellow streetlamps.

What a town. Animals, ghosts, ballerinas, fiends: They *all* get candy!

Not even the Wolf Pack lurking in Platte Park can do much to tarnish this community. See Brill down there? The big kid with the spray-paint canister? Incriminating

Spy Zoom photos of his vandalistic fun will hit the Internet in about three hours.

Yes, though the streets are crawling with monsters tonight, there never was a safer place, as places go, than Carrolton.

But no place is perfect.

Questionable characters always lurk on the outskirts or in the shadows.

For example: Who is that dark figure over by the Soccer Complex? What is that in his hands? (If indeed those things are hands.) Whoever he is, he must be watched. Fortunately, just two blocks east up the street sits a blue Toyota Avalon.

Now pan over the woods. You can't hear it from this high up, but inside the Stoneship warehouse, something is beeping. From way up here, only the author knows what it is.

But he'll give you this special, one-time-only, secret insider tip:

It's the Omega Link. *Surprise!*

On its display screen, a new message is appearing, letter by letter:

M3 SERVERS DESTROYED
GAME DOWN NATIONWIDE
WELL DONE, BIXBYS
V.

Then, with another beep, the message disappears. Nobody ever sees it . . . except you and me.